Two for Tee

Two for Tee
A GOLF STORY

by Tony Rosa

 Jackpot PRESS

Two for Tee
Copyright © 2010 by Anthony J. Rosa

"Two for Tee" may be purchased through booksellers or by contacting:
Jackpot Press
P.O. Box 594
Ft. Lauderdale, FL 33302-0594
or
JackpotPress@gmail.com

This is a work of fiction. All of the characters, names, incidents, places,
organizations, and dialogue in this novel are either the products
of the author's imagination or are used fictitiously.

ISBN: 978-0-9828225-6-2

Library of Congress Control Number: 2010930927

Printed in the United States of America

"I don't need a friend who changes when I change and who nods when I nod; my shadow does that much better."

—Plutarch

age 10

Chad Ashworth, Jr. woke still hazy among the beeping monitors and dripping hoses of the hospital room. He remembered the nurses lifting him into the bed and a few blurry exchanges with his parents, but he couldn't recall how many times he'd dozed off. Looking left, he saw his mom clinging to the side of the bed and his dad standing behind her. The starched pillowcase rubbed at the back of his ears like a fine grade of sandpaper. From darkness framed in the window, he knew nighttime had fallen. His legs, wrapped in miles of bandages, felt alien. He didn't have the strength to move them.

"Well, hello sleepyhead," his mom said.

Chad tried to speak with a parched mouth. "How long have I been out?"

"Just a couple of hours."

His dad smiled. "Your longest stretch yet."

She leaned closer. "You want some water?"

Chad nodded and started to sit up.

She patted the blankets. "Stay flat."

Chad took a few sips from a straw then sank his head back into the pillow. *If only I had a chance to start the day over,* he thought. *If only I had stood somewhere else.* It all happened so fast. *If only I had finished my chores.* Chad looked over to his dad. "Did you check on the fish?"

"Don't you remember?" His dad's smile looked artificial. "I told you earlier that we called Aunt Paula. She's going to stop by the house and make sure they're okay."

"Don't worry about that," his mom said.

Chad thought, *How could I help but not worry?* Parts of the afternoon flashed back to him. Wilting in a strange bed, stricken from physical damage and mental trauma, he worried about many things. *Will I ever run and jump again? Will my skin grow back? Will I ever walk again?* He couldn't remember if he had already asked these questions. Since no answers came to mind, he decided to ask again. Tears leaked from his eyes. "Am I ever gonna be a normal kid again?"

"Of course you are," his mom said.

Chad couldn't detect any signs of fatigue in her voice or on her face. A mask appeared to hide hours of fret.

His dad, still wearing the dental lab coat from a routine day, remained planted behind her. "Don't even think such things."

Using her thumb, his mom rubbed the tears from Chad's cheek. "The doctor said ten-year-old boys heal fast."

Chad wanted to believe her, but the few glimpses of his damaged legs were horrifying.

"You're a real fighter, champ," his dad preached like an ineffectual coach down thirty points at halftime.

Chad touched the hose feeding oxygen to his nose. "How's Buzzy?"

"He's gonna be fine," she said while glancing towards the window. "They're looking him over now."

Chad felt groggy as the painkilling medicine pumped through his veins. He closed his eyes once more to drift into pleasant darkness. Before dozing off, he thought he heard his dad whisper to his mom, "Tell me again how it happened."

* * *

Buzzy Odom sat in a state of stunned silence unable to control the nervous energy that shook his leg. For some reason, he thought about passengers tossed from the *Titanic* as they bobbed on rolling waves. Whenever the nurse appeared from behind a door and called the next name, he imagined her reciting from a passenger list. He reached up to feel the spiky ends of the singed hairs on his head and breathed a sigh of relief that no pangs of pain accompanied the exploration. He repositioned his arms around his mother's midsection gripping it like a life preserver. His heel tapped on the polished floor, sending an echo through the waiting room.

"Sit still," his mom said, "you're shaking my chair."

"Sorry."

When the door swung open again, Buzzy squirmed. The nurse announced another name and he watched someone else disappear behind the door.

His mom pulled a small mirror from her purse. She looked into it and adjusted her hair. "I didn't even have time to put on makeup," she said in a low voice. "When am I ever gonna be able to not worry about you boys?"

Buzzy heard the question many times before and knew to remain quiet.

The nurse reappeared at the doorway and called another name.

"Your older brother Wayne," his mom said, "I expect he would pull such a stunt. But not you. What gave you such an idea?"

Buzzy looked at the floor. "I don't know." Thoughts swam in his head: *Why did Chad kick the cup? If only he'd stood still. Do I have to tell Dad? Chad's gonna be okay.* The leg twitching grew faster.

After ten minutes, Buzzy gave up on hearing his name. He released the grip and began thumbing through a magazine.

"Buzzy Odom," a nurse announced. He dropped the magazine and floated through the door. "I'll put you in room number eight," the nurse said. "Hop up here," she said to Buzzy. "The doctor will be in to see you soon."

Buzzy sat on the exam table swinging his legs. As the minutes multiplied, he looked over to his mother. "How much longer?"

"For the third time," she said. "I don't know."

Buzzy stared out the door and wondered about his fate.

Behind a wave of nurses, his dad drifted into the doorway. Raindrops stained the shoulders of his light blue uniform like polka dots. Buzzy imagined a hissing radiator in an overheated car. Any wrong move and his dad could blow.

"Jerry," his mom said with a deep exhale.

Buzzy's dad grumbled, "What happened?"

His mom remained quiet.

"Okay," he said for a second time. "What happened?"

Buzzy felt her arm around his shoulder. She patted his back. "Go ahead," she said, "tell him."

Buzzy stretched his mouth wide for the words, "Well—." He looked at the blurry tiles on the floor. He gasped for air, "Uh-uh well—."

"Go ahead," his dad said. "Get on with it."

Buzzy's leg twitched. "Well, uh, see—." The saliva in his mouth thickened and became sticky between his lips. "I, uh, lit this fire. See. I got the lighter fluid. See? Uh-uh, and it went higher, and Chad uh-uh, caught on fire."

His dad roared, "You're not making any sense."

Buzzy stared at the blurry steel-toed work shoes on the tile floor. "Uh, I said—," He buried his face into his mother's midsection and broke into an all-out bawl.

His mom's voice became higher pitched. "It's okay."

Buzzy held her tight.

She draped her arm around his shoulders. "Don't you know any better?"

By the time an emergency room doctor entered the room, Buzzy had calmed down. The doctor asked some routine questions followed by a quick examination. "Those eyebrows will grow back," he said. "Beyond that, you look to be okay."

"Okay?" Buzzy's dad raised his voice. "Once we get home, he may have another reason to come back and see you."

After the doctor left, Buzzy closed his eyes and buried his head into his mother's midsection. He heard his dad ask, "How's the other boy?"

"We don't know yet," his mom said, "but he's a little worse off."

"Great," his dad said. "We haven't been in the new house a month and we're already sending neighborhood kids to the hospital." The muffled voice of his dad continued, "What a great way to meet the new neighbors."

Buzzy's leg started shaking again.

* * *

Days later, a doctor knocked on the door and entered Chad's room. Without looking at anyone in particular he said, "How we doing?" He reached for a clipboard hanging from the wall. He flipped open the metal cover and tapped down a list with a ballpoint pen.

Chad's mom neared the doctor. "That's the same question we want to ask you," she said. "How *are* we doing?"

As the doctor inspected the bandages, Chad remained frozen in position. *Surely*, he thought, *he'll notice some improvement. I followed instructions; I've kept the legs absolutely still since the last inspection.*

"It's still early," the doctor said. "But everything looked good the last time we changed the bandages. Our main concerns at this stage are dehydration and infection. We'll focus on keeping the burned areas clean and we'll continue to remove any dead tissue. The medications will help relieve pain and prevent infection."

Chad looked over to his dad.

"We wanted to ask you something," his dad said.

"Go ahead."

"I know it's not that important now, but we didn't know what to think." He tilted his head toward Chad, "He's been asking us about playing sports, and I said we'd have to talk to you about that."

"Oh, I'm afraid contact sports will be out of the question for a few years," the doctor said, looking straight at Chad. "The burns severely damaged the skin on your legs. Any unnecessary trauma could set back the healing process."

Chad exhaled and shrank deeper into the bed.

His dad tried to clarify the directive. "But that doesn't mean all sports, does it?"

"No," the doctor said. "Not necessarily. As a matter of fact, to heal properly, you'll be put through a pretty rigorous exercise routine."

Chad decided to speak up. "But, um, sports are important."

"Don't worry," the doctor said. "There are plenty of other sports you might like to try. The doctor scratched his head. "What about golf?"

"Golf?"

"Sure," the doctor said. "Golf is a great sport. If you want my opinion, I'd say the best sport for those two legs would be golf."

*   *   *

Buzzy stood in the doorway and rubbed his itchy eyes. He tried to avoid smells of medicine and sights of patients in the hallways by holding his breath and focusing on the shiny floor. When his mom knocked on the open door, he sighed with exhaustion and moved like a snail. For two straight nights, fireballs jolted him awake. They devoured every person he knew.

"Look who's here," Chad's dad said, lowering the volume on the television. "It's Buzzarino and his mom."

The visit weighed on Buzzy's nerves with the same dread found outside the principal's office. At times, he pictured Chad in a grave state. Other times, he envisioned a miracle healing. Either way, he prepared for the truth. *"You make sure you apologize to that boy,"* his father's directive echoed in his brain. *"And you better treat him so nice that they don't ever decide to sue us."*

Chad's dad motioned with a wave. "Come on in."

Glued to his mother's side, Buzzy stared around the room. Machines beeped at intervals, numbers flashed on monitors, and long graphs of paper hung from slots. Hoses drained tanks and bags dripped liquid. Tubes and wires hurdled the bed railing and stabbed into Chad.

Buzzy fought the urge to cry.

No words would come out.

His mom nudged him. "Say hello."

He said, "Huh-h-hey Chad."

Chad reached for the bedside controls and began moving the mattress. "Check out this wicked bed," he said as if confinement in the apparatus was an envious adventure.

Buzzy never heard him use the word *wicked*. Relief flowed through his veins. The anxiety began to melt away. Chad didn't ignore him. He didn't appear angry. Better still, he used his favorite word. Buzzy feigned a nervous laugh. "Pretty cool."

"Check out this button," Chad said. His eyes widened as the bed moved in different directions.

Buzzy looked up to see Chad's parents exchange a long glance. "We're gonna get a cup of coffee in the cafeteria," Chad's mom said, dabbing at her watery eyes. "Would you like to join us Sally?"

"Sure."

Chad's mom continued, "You kids want anything?"

"No, but thanks," Chad said.

Buzzy shook his head.

The adults headed to the cafeteria.

"Watch what this one does," Chad said, continuing with the buttons.

Within minutes, Buzzy reverted to his old self. "Let me try it."

Chad handed over the controls.

As he steered, Buzzy added sound effects.

Chad's smile warmed the room.

With a receptive audience, Buzzy decided to continue with a few jokes. "Wanna hear a joke?"

Buzzy offered a few lame riddles before recalling the main purpose of his visit. The voice lingered in his head, *"You make sure you apologize to that boy."* At first, Buzzy felt flush. His upper lip quivered. "Chad," he took in a deep breath and looked to the floor. "I'm, uh, I'm sorry." Hearing no initial response, Buzzy looked up.

The sun lit Chad's face as he gazed toward the window. He turned toward Buzzy. "Don't worry," he said. "It was an accident."

Buzzy's arms dangled at his side. "Hey," he perked up as he felt the heavy load of guilt getting lighter. "I brought you something." Digging into his back pocket, he pulled out a slingshot his older brother Wayne fashioned from a Y-shaped tree branch. Only days before, he and Chad took turns firing pebbles at an empty soda can with the gadget. Buzzy extended the peace offering. "Here."

Chad adjusted the bed to a more-upright position. "Your slingshot?"

"You can have it."

"Thanks," Chad said. He aimed in the air and mustered enough strength to pull the rubber strips halfway.

*   *   *

"It's sure nice to be home," Chad said as he swung his bandaged legs from the car. His mom handed him crutches. He looked toward the front door and said, "Did someone paint the house?"

"Nope," she said. "Maybe we cleaned up a little."

"It just looks different." Chad stuck the foam-padded stumps in his armpits and grabbed the handles. As he wobbled from the car, the rubber stoppers at the ends of each crutch thumped at the sidewalk.

"You know," his mom said, "we're here to help."

"I know," said Chad, "I just wanted to prove I could do it."

As Chad reached the porch steps, his dad picked him up and carried him through the open door and up the stairs. Sweat dripped from his dad's forehead. When they reached the bed, he exhaled. "Whew!"

"Well, don't worry about coming downstairs for a long time," his mother said. "I'll be bringing your meals, and look. We moved a T.V. in here for you."

Chad nodded and smiled. "Thanks."

"And look by your nightstand," his dad said, resting his hands on his hips. "Just ring that bell if you need anything."

"Okay."

"Just get comfortable," his mom said, "and I'll be back in a few minutes to check on you."

"Thanks." Chad reclined and stared at the ceiling.

His mom yelled from downstairs, "We'll wash the *Super Socks* later."

Chad wore a flesh-colored garment on his legs. The elastic leggings applied the same amount of pressure as healthy skin. His mom called the special clothing his *Super Socks* and promised they gave him special strength. Doctors instructed he wear the *Super Socks* twenty-three hours a day for eighteen straight months.

Flat on his back with his legs inclined, the view from his bed remained the same for days. Often, he broke into a sweat from the warmth. Other times, a stack of blankets could not keep him from shivering. Constant boredom filled the room as days of confinement dragged on. He watched shadows creep across his floor in the morning and the light fade from his windows at night. Cartoons and an occasional game show poured from the television.

Being in a sterile environment for so long, Chad developed a keen sense of smell. He caught a whiff of mildew accompanying his dad as he entered the bedroom early one evening.

"Check this out," his dad said, pointing to a set of junior golf clubs draped over one shoulder. The small bag made him look like a giant.

Chad swung his legs from bed. "What's that?"

"Golf clubs."

Chad put a book aside. "Where'd ya' get um?"

"It's a funny story," his dad said. "Wanna hear it?"

"Sure."

"Okay," he removed the small bag from his shoulder. The irons rattled as he leaned them into a corner. "So I was in the office the other day talking with my partner, you know, Dr. Mike, and we got to talking about sports. We started to talk about golf and he was telling me how much he loves golf. You remember seeing the pictures in his office? You know the ones of him out on the golf course, and the ones with him in a group before they played in a tournament?"

Chad answered. "Um, I remember."

"Well, he just goes on-and-on about how great golf is," his dad said. "And, finally, I say to him, 'You know, I think I'm gonna start playing golf again.'

"So he gets all excited and says, 'That would be great.' He goes on-and-on about how we could be partners in these golf tournaments for dentists and then he says to me, 'Hey, I got something for you.'

"A few days later he comes into my office with this set of golf clubs," he pointed at the bag of clubs resting in the corner. "And he says, 'I think you may want these for Chad. They've been sitting in my garage for years collecting dust. Both my boys learned how to play golf using them. They're not doing anybody any good just sitting in my garage.'

"So, I thanked him and brought the clubs home."

Chad smiled and nodded. As soon as his dad left the room, he hobbled over and withdrew each club for inspection. He found some golf balls in a zippered compartment and placed one on the carpeted floor. Using the putter, he stroked the ball toward a leg at the foot of his bed. Within days, he was hitting the post eight out of ten tries.

age 11

For months, Chad's bicycle sat idle in the garage. The only visible parts were the handlebars and seat peeking above dusty boxes. A cool weekend in the fall got Chad feeling strong enough for a ride, so he dug it out. As he rolled the bike toward the sunlight, he noticed the rear tire had gone flat.

It reminded Chad of his legs.

Months of an excruciating regiment wore on Chad and deflated his confidence. On the bad days, he looked at his legs and felt disconnected. When he shed the *Super Socks* for washing each day, the lower limbs appeared strange. Chad almost believed they belonged to someone else. When asleep, he reclaimed the old legs in his dreams. When awake, he wished the whole ordeal only existed in a simple nightmare.

Chad propped the bicycle against a workbench and went inside the house. He found his dad watching television. "Um, dad," he said. "I went to, um, get my bike in the garage, and, it like, has a flat tire."

"Slow down," his dad said while lowering the footrest on the recliner. "Let's take a look."

Chad eased through the first day of school although a handful of kids grew jealous of the extra attention he received. Within days, they made him an object for ridicule launching hallway sneers and snickers. Chad became quiet in social situations. While his brain searched for the right words, a string of 'ums' often sputtered from his mouth. Other times, 'like' filled the same voids. Both words comforted his speech like a security blanket.

Often, his parents corrected Chad when he rambled with 'ums' and 'likes' with a simple, *"Slow down."*

"It's flat all right," Chad's dad said after assessing the rear wheel. The metal rim dug into the flattened rubber as he pushed it inside. "Let's pump some air back in it." He grabbed the pump hanging from a hook on the wall, screwed the hose onto the valve stem, and cranked the handle. "Let's give it a few minutes to see if there are any leaks."

Chad grew accustomed to waiting. The accident itself had not changed him as much as the extended period of healing and the uncertainty of the future. On the good days during recovery, he accepted the new look of his legs. What meant normal before, he decided, changed into something different. Chad envisioned worse possibilities. He remembered several other patients in rehabilitation suffering from far more gruesome injuries. On the good days, Chad counted his blessings.

"Well," his dad said as they re-inspected the tire, "looks like we got ourselves a bona fide leak."

"Um, can you fix it?"

"Why, you're looking at the fastest bicycle repair guy in the neighborhood," his dad said with such authority, "as long as I can find a good assistant."

Chad smiled. "I can do that."

"Grab the toolbox on the bench over there and we'll get the wheel off."

With both hands full of tools, Chad stood nearby.

His dad loosened the rear axle nuts and pulled the deflated tire from the frame.

Chad watched as his dad extracted the inner tube from inside the knobby tire and dunked it into a tub filled with water. The inner tube was vital; it held the air.

"This is how you find the leak," his dad said. "Keep your eye out for air bubbles."

Chad remembered similar submersions during his rehabilitation.

"Right there," Chad said, spotting a trail of bubbles.

"Yep," his dad said and grabbed Chad's finger. "Hold it right here so we'll know where to put the patch."

His dad worked like a physical therapist. Chad caught a whiff of rubber cement as he watched him secure a patch. It dried within seconds. His dad inserted the inner tube, pried the tire onto the wheel, and refilled it with air. "There," he said, "that oughta hold her."

Just as Chad hopped on the bicycle, his mother entered the garage. She looked as if she smelled a foul odor. "I was wondering what the two of you were up to."

"We've been fixing a flat tire," his dad said.

Creases in her forehead appeared in shaky lines. "Well that's okay, but I hope no one is planning on taking a bicycle ride anytime soon."

"Please, Mom," Chad said, "I'll, um, be real careful."

"Sorry buddy," she said, standing with folded arms. "What if you have a wreck and skin your knee? I just don't think you should be riding yet. You need to wait a few more months before you can get on that again."

Chad looked over to his father.

"I guess she's right pal," his dad said, shrugging his shoulders and tilting his head to one side. "I wasn't thinking."

The bicycle ride had to wait.

* * *

Just before a fork full of mashed potatoes reached his mouth, the clutches of a hairy forearm and taut bicep wrapped around Buzzy's neck. It felt like a boa constrictor. With his head caught in the vise grip, bony knuckles dug into his scalp and knocked on his skull. Before Buzzy had a chance to retaliate, Wayne released his grip and escaped to a separate chair. Buzzy wiped his mouth with one hand and tamped down his mussed hair with the other. He lapped up the playful attention like a smiling puppy.

Sometimes he loved his older brother.

Buzzy's dad, still wearing his soiled uniform from a warehouse workday, sat at the head of the table. He glared at Wayne. "Where you been?"

"Nowhere," Wayne said, "just running late."

Buzzy's mom, having already delivered a platter of meatloaf, a bowl of mashed potatoes and a dish of corn to the table, settled into her chair. As she passed a basket of bread around the table, she attempted to serve up some conversation. "So, how was everyone's day?"

Wayne scraped the bowl of corn empty and placed it near an ashtray full of squashed-out cigarette butts. The sweet smell of baked tomato sauce from the crusty meatloaf hovered over the table.

With his plate overrunning, Buzzy's dad grabbed a nearby shaker and peppered everything until it looked sooty. "Are you animals deaf?" His roar broke the silence. "Your mother asked a question."

Wayne wiggled like an eel from his slouching position. "I'm finding my way around all right." He grabbed a roll from the basket. "I've met a few people."

"Well," Buzzy's mom said. "I worry about you Wayne. I know you try real hard and sometimes you're not treated fair. But I hope this will be a new beginning for you; a clean slate. Are your classes okay?"

Wayne hesitated and said, "Yeah."

"Are you making it on time?"

"Yeah."

"Well, I hope you'll know better than to be late. You should be concerned with getting your diploma."

Wayne twirled his fork in the air as if to say, *'Whoop-de-do.'*

"This could be a fresh start for you Wayne," she said.

"Whatever."

To Buzzy, Wayne did no wrong. When people claimed Wayne broke the rules, he was really being adventurous. When teachers said he was being lazy, he was really demonstrating independence. And, when the principal said he was being disrespectful, he was really being a rebel. Buzzy wanted to be like Wayne. He followed him around and copied his every move. He did anything for his brother's attention and approval.

Buzzy's dad shook his head.

His mom turned her attention. "How about you, Buzzy?"

"Me and Chad are in the same class," Buzzy said.

"That's nice."

"We walk together to the bus stop every morning."

"You better be nice to that kid," Buzzy's dad said for the hundredth time. "You better be so nice to that kid that he forgets what you did."

Buzzy's eyes watered. He lowered his head.

His dad turned to his mother. "Have they ever said anything about suing us?"

"Oh, my," she said. "Do you have to bring that up at the dinner table?"

"Well, yeah." He stuffed a fork loaded with meatloaf into his mouth.

"The Ashworths are fine people," she said. "Not once have they ever mentioned the accident."

"If they wanted to, they could take everything we have."

"Well, like I said, I don't think they will," she said. "You know, you could make more of an effort in talking to Dr. Ashworth."

"You'll never catch me going near any dentist," he said, gathering mashed potatoes onto a piece of meat. "They cause me too much pain."

The boys laughed.

Buzzy fed on the laughter. "I heard a joke today." He sat taller and looked around the table. "Wanna hear it?"

No one responded.

Not deterred by their indifference, Buzzy forged ahead. "Where does the *Lone Ranger* take his garbage?"

Everyone kept eating except Buzzy's mom. "Where?"

Buzzy wanted full attention from the audience. He looked around the table. "Everybody give up?" They ignored him. He broke the silence by singing in tune with the *Lone Ranger* television theme music, "To the dump, to the dump, to the dump, dump, dump."

Wayne gave him a smirk. "That's old as the dinosaurs."

"Well," Buzzy said happy at least someone paid attention, "I never heard it before."

Buzzy took two large gulps of milk. The liquid cooled the back of his throat and drained into his stomach. He gasped for air and chugged the milk until the glass was empty. Buzzy thought, *Maybe a little physical comedy was what this crowd needed.* He blasted a loud burp, "Baaaaaahhhh." To cover his tracks he said, "Excuse me."

Again, no one laughed.

"Buzzy," his mom said. "Don't you know any better?"

He canceled the rest of the show. *Sometimes the audience just didn't get it.* Buzzy tried to get off the stage with a little dignity. "I said excuse me."

His mom looked over to her husband. "Do you see what kind of example you are?"

"Don't blame me," Buzzy's dad said without looking up from his plate. He pushed back his chair and undid his belt buckle. He retrieved a pack of cigarettes from his shirt pocket and pulled the ashtray in front of him. He lit a cigarette, exhaled the smoke, and sat the burning stick into an ashtray slot.

Buzzy's mom tried to restart the conversation. "Buzzy's been a good friend to Chad," she said. "He's been over there almost every day. He spends most afternoons watching T.V. with Chad and playing games."

"Sounds like he's your girlfriend," Wayne said with a sneer.

Buzzy growled like a bulldog. "Shut up Wayne."

His mom ignored the banter. "Buzzy's been a real good friend," she said.

"Well, you better," his dad said. "They'll sue us for everything."

"Yeah, scroat," Wayne piled on, "they'll sue us for everything." He pointed a knife smeared with butter at him.

"Shut up Wayne," Buzzy said.

Sometimes Buzzy hated his older brother.

* * *

Chad ripped through wrapped boxes and tissue paper only to discover clothes. From the shredded gift-wrap, he lifted a pair of knickers, argyle socks, and a vest. A matching cap the shape of a pancake wilted atop the vest.

His mom put on a smile. "It's golf clothes."

Chad held the garments with the tips of his fingers. Scientists handled radioactive material with higher regard. "Um, okay." Chad nodded with a smirk.

"Go try 'em on." She tried to hold them next to him to be certain of the size.

As he climbed the stairs, Chad reflected on the changes in his mom. Banning the bicycle ride came as no surprise. Chad could have predicted it. From the beginning of his recuperation, she developed a pattern of going overboard. She insisted he take a nap when he wasn't even tired. Instead of changing the bandages once daily as suggested, she swapped them out twice. When asked to provide plenty of liquids, she dispatched enough water through his system to drown a fish. When the doctor advised to stay away from contact sports for a few years, she decided it meant a lifetime ban.

His mom yelled from the back door, "Come on outside. I want to take your picture."

With slumping shoulders and dragging feet, Chad skulked outdoors and stood next to the bag of clubs already waiting in the backyard. The baggy knickers and argyle socks covered the *Super Socks*.

"He looks like a newsboy standing on a sidewalk with a stack of papers," his dad said.

Chad kicked at the ground.

"You're not helping the situation," his mom said.

But his dad continued. "You should yell out, 'Extra! Extra! Read all about it!'"

Chad couldn't control a grin that leaked out.

"Now look up here and smile," she said, aiming a camera in his direction.

Chad glared.

"You look so cute," she said. "Please smile."

Chad started to take off the clothes before his mom had a chance to advance the film for another shot. "I would never wear this out in public," he said, "not even on *Halloween*."

Chad's mom looked at his dad and curled her lip. "Even when I try to do something special," she said, "it flops."

*   *   *

"Just relax," his dad advised. "Slow down, and take a deep breath." He joked that pulling teeth was easier than giving golf advice.

A string of bad shots unfolded. Chad whined, "Why I am not getting any better?"

"You're doing fine," his dad offered while sitting in a lawn chair. "You have to be patient. It's going to take a while." As he shifted his weight trying to emphasize a pointer for the next swing, the aluminum frame squeaked. "Try and turn your hips a little more."

Chad made a good swing and sent the ball flying. He felt better.

"That's it!" his dad said, "Attaboy!"

Golf occupied Chad's thoughts. During the countless days he spent lying in bed, his eyes often wandered to the set of junior clubs leaning in the corner. He imagined traipsing across emerald fields on healthy legs. It took him away from the grueling rehabilitation routine and filled the lonely hours of recovery.

Chad first became proficient stroking golf balls across the carpeted floor with the putter. He requested and received a plug-in gadget that looked like the business end of a dustpan. Upon hitting one of the numbered slots, gravity pulled the ball to the lowest point triggering an electronic peg that kicked it back. His mother decided it would save time tracking back-and-forth to retrieve the ball. Assuming he reached the target, Chad found it worked great about half the time.

Like his recovery, learning to play golf was not easy. In most other sports, going faster, harder, and quicker gave you an edge. Chad learned that same aggressive approach wrecked the golfer. No matter how frustrating, he never wavered from a positive attitude. Maybe because, deep down, he knew golf was the only option.

Whenever Chad remembered making lay-ups on the basketball court, he now imagined making tap-in putts on the green. When he recalled the times he exploded off the line of scrimmage in football, he pictured instead exploding shots from sand bunkers. And when he remembered how he once fielded ground balls and tossed them over to first base, he now envisioned lobbing chip shots to an elevated green and watching them roll toward the cup.

His dad fidgeted to find comfort. "You didn't follow-through on that one."

"I know." Chad slumped and shook his head.

"Check your alignment. Make sure you're aiming at something."

"I know."

After a good shot, Chad looked to him and smiled.

"You're really tagging that driver today."

A few swings later Chad topped one off the tee and slammed his club to the ground. "Uuuggghhh."

"Looked up on that one," his dad said.

"Um, was it my take-away?"

His dad squirmed. "It looks okay to me."

Chad's frustration grew as the golf shots got worse.

"You know what buddy," his dad said. "We may need some help with this." He scratched his head and said, "And I know just the guy to call."

*   *   *

"Let us sally forth," Chad said to Buzzy.

Buzzy looked confused. "Who's Sally?"

"It's what they're always saying in this book I'm reading, *Don Quixote*. When they setout for an adventure, they sally forth."

"You read books in the summertime?"

"Yeah."

"When you don't have to?"

"Yeah, it's better than the movies if you think about it."

"Whatever."

Chad pushed through the backdoor of his house and said to his mom, "Can me and Buzzy walk to the *S.D.I.*?"

She repeated the request. "Can you and Buzzy walk to the *S.D.I.*?"

"Yeah, um, Buzzy does it all the time."

"He does?"

"Yeah, it's not that far."

"Why do you want to go?" She rubbed the creases in her forehead. "What do you need?"

"Um, we want to get a *Slushie*."

"Well—," she said, looking around the room as if hoping to find an excuse, "—I don't know." She started to pick-up the phone but removed her hand from the receiver. "You've got one hour," she said. "If you're not home in one hour, I'm getting in the car to come look for you."

Chad almost jumped. "No problem!"

"Go straight there and come straight home," she said, pointing her index finger. "And stay on the main road. If I have to come look for you in the car, I better be able to find you on the main road."

Chad would have agreed to any terms. "Yes ma'am."

As they setout for the Super Drive-In convenient store, the sun loomed high and warmed the tops of Chad's shoulders. Within minutes, home disappeared from sight and the adventure felt like an exploration. Chad strolled on the graveled shoulder of the road kicking at the occasional pebble trying to free it from the underlying gooey tar. He traveled facing the traffic as promised and slowed his pace and moved in single file when cars approached. The smell of fresh cut grass reached his nose as they hiked past a front yard filled with roaring mowers of a lawn service. Two houses later, the noise level weakened enough for conversation.

Buzzy moved sideways with scissor steps. "Whatta you gonna git?"

"Um, I don't know yet," said Chad not ready to commit to anything before all the options were in front of him. "Probably some baseball cards."

Buzzy pivoted and marched backwards. "I got a joke for you."

"Okay."

"So this guy goes into a pizza shop and orders a large pizza, okay?"

"Okay."

"And the guy behind the counter asks him if he wants to cut the pizza into eight slices or twelve, okay?"

"Okay."

"So the guy says, 'you better make it eight slices, I'm not hungry enough to eat twelve slices.'"

Chad smiled.

"You get it?" Buzzy often explained his jokes. "It's the same amount of pizza no matter how many slices."

"I got it," Chad said. "Pretty funny."

"That's why you're my friend," Buzzy said. "You always get my jokes."

Houses, street signs, trees, ditches, all seen a million times from the car window appeared familiar, but up close they made a different impression.

Buzzy pointed at a broken broom handle rising from a curbside pile of trash. He grabbed the exposed end and pulled it from the heap. "Check this out."

Its apparent value puzzled Chad. "Whatta you gonna do with it?"

"My brother can make a pair of nunchucks out of it." Buzzy twirled the broomstick. "All you gotta do is cut it right here—," Buzzy used his flat hand as if it were a saw, "—and connect these two pieces with a rope."

"Oh."

As the strides piled up, long pants that covered the *Super Socks* heated Chad like a portable sauna. Sweat trailed around his eyebrows and streamed down his cheeks. As they passed another house, he watched with envy as young kids took turns hopping over a sprinkler. Some of them wore bathing suits while others let their summer clothes soak in the spray. If any of them got too close to the sprinkler, they screamed as the laser-thin stream near the nozzle stung the skin.

Chad watched as an older boy snuck up with a separate hose, ready to launch a surprise attack. While most of the kids ran from the spray, one brave boy stood firm, as if he welcomed the drenching. Chad thought about *Don Quixote* and imagined the two lads as knights at a jousting tournament.

The broken end of the broomstick made a static noise as Buzzy drug it through the gravel. "Check out this line," Buzzy said. "If we get lost, we can look for this line on the way home."

"Okay," Chad agreed, but doubted they would get lost.

"Keep your eye out for bottles," Buzzy instructed. "We can cash 'em in."

They split up to explore both sides of the road. Chad surveyed the side facing traffic as promised, while Buzzy checked the other.

After unearthing a second bottle, Buzzy abandoned the broomstick. "I can pick it up on the way home."

By the time they reached the store, they had collected two empties apiece.

As he entered the automatic door of the convenient store, Chad swallowed in the comfort of air conditioning. He quickly gazed at the candy rack that filled the entire front wall. Colored logos wrapped around the metal rack fronts with a full box of matching candy resting behind. A whole afternoon could be spent mesmerized by the temple of treats.

"SweetTarts are my favorite," Buzzy said, licking his lips.

Chad remembered how Buzzy nibbled around the slobber-soaked edges of the edible hockey-puck candy until it shrank enough to fit in his mouth. The side of his cheek would remain swollen until it dissolved.

"You gotta see this," Buzzy said to Chad like a seasoned tour guide. He pointed toward a box of candy and said, "Check this out!"

Chad's mouth watered. The selection overloaded him. "Oh yeah, I love those."

Buzzy grabbed two packs of SweetTarts and headed for the counter.

Chad wandered around the store. As he approached the insulated glass doors of the refrigerators, he noticed a concave mirror hanging from the ceiling. He looked in the mirror and saw his skewed image. At first, he waved his arms to test if the reflection responded in similar fashion. Once it did, his thoughts turned to golf. Chad turned and took a stance as if addressing a golf ball. In slow motion, he watched for the position of his arms, shoulders, and hands as they performed an imaginary swing. Not liking what he saw with the first swing, Chad kept staring into the concave mirror as he took another stance and swing. With no one watching, he continued until the swing repeated itself like a machine.

Returning to the candy rack, Chad remembered the reason for the quest: baseball cards. He went straight to the cardboard box and grabbed a couple of packs hoping they contained another copy of his favorite player or any of those still missing from his collection. He placed them on the counter and ordered a blueberry *Slushie*.

"I saw you back there—," the cashier said to him while handing over the frozen drink, "—in the mirror." He pointed to the surveillance mirror hanging from the ceiling. "You know I've watched many a suspicious character in that mirror. But I have to tell you, you're the first pint-sized golfer I ever seen."

Chad smiled and took his change. Outside the door, he ripped into the first pack and stuck the powdered-sugar-coated piece of gum into his mouth. The hard stick tasted like cardboard and shattered into pieces as he bit into it. He shuffled through cards and reported his findings, "Another checklist. I hate checklists. I like, get one every time."

On the way home, Chad remained on the graveled shoulder while Buzzy crisscrossed swales like a downhill skier maneuvering flags. They made random stops to investigate anthills, chase June bugs, and to peer at a cat hiding in a culvert. Noticing a kickball resting in the bottom of a ditch, Chad watched as Buzzy punted it.

As they neared home, Chad saw his mom waving from the window.

He waved back.

"See you later," Buzzy said, heading across the street. The crumpled bag of potato chips he carried for his mom looked like they fell off a moving train.

"I'm home," Chad dragged through the back door.

He drank in the cool air as he climbed the stairs to his room. For the first time since the accident, his mother allowed him to do something normal. Although exhausted, he made the roundtrip excursion to the Super Drive-In without any problems. The long pants and *Super Socks* slowed him down, but didn't stop him.

That night, Chad skipped his usual exercises. He figured the legs stretched enough. He felt as battered and beaten as *Don Quixote* after fighting over a spittoon he thought was a magical helmet.

*   *   *

Chad stood next to the open trunk as the winter wind stung his eyes. He looked down the tree-lined drive they traveled and noticed the spacious homes situated on expansive, manicured lawns. After driving through the brick columns that held open the wrought-iron gate, he now knew what existed on the other side of the well-trimmed hedge.

"Let me get those for you sir," the attendant said as if it would be an insult for them to lift their golf bags.

"Okay," Chad's dad said. "We're here to meet with Joe Doaks."

"Yessir," said the uniformed attendant. "Mr. Doaks asked me to keep an eye out for you. He's waiting in the pro-shop." He pointed toward the brick building with large windows, "Right through that door."

The attendant pulled off with their clubs in his charge.

Chad's dad looked over to him. "You may want to bring that extra sweater."

Chad reached into the back seat and grabbed the additional sweater that, thanks to his mom, matched his long corduroy pants. As they strode toward the pro-shop, his pants sounded like someone playing a ridged percussion instrument. Beneath the long pants, Chad wore the *Super Socks* for warmth.

Outside the pro-shop door, Chad's dad pointed at the ground. "Check this out." He swiped the bottom of his golf shoes over upturned brush bristles.

Although Chad kept his cleats immaculate, he took a turn in case anything offensive adhered to the soles from the parking lot. He entered the warmth of the pro-shop with the assurance he wouldn't sully the carpet.

"Hey *Stretch*," said a tall man whose smiling white teeth contrasted with his tanned face. He returned a putter to the display rack and extended his hand. "How's the golf game?"

Chad's dad shook hands and slapped him on the back, "It's full of long stretches of mediocrity, occasionally interrupted by flashes of brilliance, and soaked with streaks of stupidity. How are the choppers?"

Chad had heard the same rehearsed answer before.

"I'm brushing and flossing five times a day."

"Well, the smile's the same, but you're gaining a few more wrinkles."

"That goes for both of us."

"I want you to meet my son," his dad said. "This is Chad, Jr."

"So you're *Stretch, Jr.*?" The man offered his hand. "My name is Joe Doaks."

"Um, nice to meet you Mr. Doaks," Chad said. Heat rushed to his face.

"Call me Joe. The only Mr. Doaks I know is my dad."

Chad stuffed his hands into his pockets and looked at the carpet.

"Let's grab a bite to eat," Joe suggested. He wrapped his arms together and faked some shivers. "I'm not use to this cold weather."

Once around the clubhouse table, the small talk revolved around golf. "I don't give a lot of lessons," Joe said. "As a professional golfer, I earn my living playing in tournaments. It's golf professionals, those that usually work at a golf course or country club, they're the experts at giving lessons and running a pro-shop."

Chad listened and remembered how to separate the two different career types by whether the word 'golf' came before or after the word 'professional'.

"Well," his dad said, "There aren't too many people in the world better at golf, and we really appreciate any help you can give us."

"*Stretch!*" Joe said with a smile. "Better go easy with the compliments."

"Yeah, yeah. I just wanted you to know how much we appreciate it."

"Listen," Joe said, "it's really my pleasure." He looked over to Chad. "You know, when I was a freshman on the basketball team, your dad was a senior."

Chad sat tall in his seat. "Um, really?"

"Yep, like most freshman, I was really lost. But, your dad looked out for me."

Chad's dad flashed a wry smile. "Joe was a better golfer in college than he was a basketball player."

"You're probably right about that," Joe said with a grin. "After your dad graduated, I stopped playing basketball all together and just concentrated on golf. But I sure loved playing basketball my freshman year. I remember sitting on the bench and cheering for the older guys like your dad. We won some big games."

Chad's dad said, "Looks like you picked the right sport."

"Yeah, the first few years were a struggle, but to make my living playing golf has been a dream come true."

Chad's confidence grew with each bite. He looked to his dad and said, "Um, why does he call you *Stretch*?"

"That was my nickname in college," he said. "I got it my first week from an older guy on the team. He called one guy *Bump* because of his acne and another guy *Slick* because of his oily hair. He called me *Stretch* because I was only five feet ten and the shortest guy on the team." He looked over to Joe, "I guess the name stuck."

"Yeah," Joe said. "But when your dad was a senior, us young guys still called him *Stretch*, but it was for another reason. We called him *Stretch* because he always went further than anyone on the team. The coach said to shoot 100 free throws after practice, your dad would shoot 200. When he said be a certain place 15 minutes early, your dad was there 30 minutes early. Stuff like that."

"And now look at me," Chad's dad said, "I've never been farther than my own home town."

Joe shook his head and gave Chad a smile. "That's not what I meant."

When they finished eating, Joe reached into his back pocket and pulled out a small booklet. "I wanted to give you this," he said, handing a copy of *The Rules of Golf* across the table to Chad. "It's the most important thing any serious golfer should have."

It felt like a birthday for Chad. "Thank you sir."

Joe said, "How can anyone play a sport if they don't know the rules?"

"Good point," his dad nodded.

Joe signed a ticket for breakfast insisting on treating his guests.

As they strolled outdoors, Chad noticed the transformation brought on by winter. Fairways and roughs appeared dead in their dormant state and matched Joe's khaki pants. Cold-weather turf grasses blanketed the tees and greens and looked like green oases against the expansive sea of light brown. Bare tree branches lost their effectiveness to curtain restrictive views. Dead leaves gathered in the deep end of the drained swimming pool and the chilly breeze whistled through the sagging sections of lowered nets on the tennis courts.

Chad discovered golf courses, not unlike the offerings in an ice cream shop, came in many varieties. He usually got a teaspoon of vanilla in a dingy paper cup offered by the par-3 course he frequented. The country club overflowed with heaping scoops of Rocky Road, Chunky Monkey, and Cookie Dough Crunch served in a silver dish between slices of bananas, smothered in butterscotch and topped with whipped cream, nuts, and a cherry on top. Even the dirt at the country club outclassed the par-3 course.

Joe pointed to a cart already loaded with their golf bags. "Hop in and we'll drive over to the practice tee."

Chad's smaller bag of clubs squeezed between the two larger ones. The professional bag, with 'JOE DOAKS' prominently stitched in the leather, contained enough compartments to store emergency rations for a small village.

"Grab your five iron," Joe said as the cart came to a halt. "If you can hit a five iron, you can hit any club."

Chad followed behind his dad as they made their way over to a stack of balls. "It's a little nippy for me," his dad said. Before even hitting one shot, he headed to the cart. "I think I'll wait 'til it warms up a bit."

"Okay," Joe said, turning his attention to Chad. "I guess it's just you and me. Let's start with the basics." He went through the aspects of a golf swing including the grip, the stance, the takeaway, the downward motion, point of contact, and the follow-through. For each puzzle piece, he added tidbits until the amount of information piled up.

Chad tried to keep it all straight in his mind. *Maybe,* he thought, *my swing was wrong all along. Maybe, all the practicing was a waste. Maybe, I'm not really good at golf.*

"All right," said Joe, "let's see you hit a few."

Excited, Chad welcomed some action. A million instructions swam in his head: *athletic stance, arms loose, left arm, push it back, aim at something, and roll your wrists.* In about one second of action, Chad had to remember and execute so much.

A disastrous first shot flopped from the tee.

Little improvement came with the second one.

"Nice and easy," his dad said from the cushioned cart seat.

"I know," Chad shot back. "It's not like I'm not trying."

His dad nodded and waved with a smile.

"Sometimes in golf," Joe said, "trying too much is not a good thing."

Chad's next shot wasn't much better. His shoulders slumped and he looked toward the ground and murmured, "How embarrassing."

"Embarassing?" said Joe. "Let me tell you a couple a things about embarrassing. First, you'll learn soon enough that no one on the golf course cares more about your performance than you do. So, you have to think: The only person I'm really disappointing is myself. Let me ask you a question, how long do you think about someone else's bad shot?"

Chad pondered it and responded, "Um, I guess not too long."

"Right," said Joe. "So, if you don't think about their bad shot that long, do you think they're thinking about your bad shot that long?"

"Um, I guess not."

"So, that's my point. Don't worry about what other people think about you or your game. Trust me. With a name that rhymes with chokes, don't you think I've heard every catcall and disparaging remark on the golf course? For some of these sportswriters, I'm a walking dream. They can't wait to throw that word at me. So what do I do? I ignore most everything they write. Positive or negative. Because, if I started to believe what they say, or worry about what they thought, I would be a basket case. So, you know what I do?"

Chad hung on every word. "What?"

"Whenever I really blow it in a tournament, I know some sportswriter will inevitably ask me if I choked just so he can rhyme my name. So, you know what I do? I don't even acknowledge my shortcomings. I stay positive. I never admit to choking. If I ever gave in once, they would ask that same question about how *Joe Doaks chokes*. Something doesn't go my way, they would say, '*Joe Doaks chokes*.' It would be so bad, that if I wore the wrong color shirt, they would say, '*Joe Doaks chokes*.' So, what I'm telling you is don't worry about what other people think. Do your best, and handle the tough situations with dignity. If the going gets tough, you know who to blame, and you don't need anyone else telling you who to blame. And if someone tries to call you a name or says you choked, just do like me and deny them the pleasure. Stay positive. Make sense?"

"Sure," Chad said, nodding his head.

"Okay, enough with the philosophy lesson," Joe said. "Let's see you hit some more."

As Chad launched golf balls, the tips and encouragement continued. As the pile of range balls shrank, Chad began hitting the ball farther and straighter.

*   *   *

Chad wanted to keep hitting golf balls until he fell over from exhaustion.

"Let's go buddy," his dad finally yelled over.

Without looking up Chad pointed skyward and said, "One more." He hit one last good one and admired it while frozen in the follow-through position.

"Hop in," Joe said. "I want you to show you my favorite golfer."

Chad leaned forward in the bench seat between the two old friends. He scanned the grounds for golfers in all directions. *Maybe it was a legend of the game, possibly someone retired from the tour,* Chad thought. *Perhaps it was a past winner of the Masters or even a U.S. Open Champion.*

They rolled down a cart path lining the first hole and made their way toward the middle of the course. Joe looked over to his dad. "So, when you gonna join the club?"

Chad's dad looked around and took a deep breath. He exhaled and said, "It's a beautiful place."

"Let me know when you're ready," Joe said. "I know I can get you in."

"Maybe soon."

"We have a great junior program here."

Chad looked up at Joe and smiled.

Joe slowed the cart as they approached a foursome. He stayed about 150 yards behind the group. "I wanted you to see my favorite golfer."

At first, Chad failed to identify anyone famous or anything unique about the foursome. They all appeared to have average skills. Chad watched in silence. An odd thing about one person in the group became evident; an older man hobbled. As he made a golf swing, it appeared the man relied on his left leg for balance and strength.

Joe explained the long pants covered an artificial limb attached at the knee. "He's my hero," he said. "He stepped on a land mine in the war. You've heard people say they'd give their right leg for something. Well, he gave his right leg for his country."

Chad's dad stated the obvious. "And he plays golf?"

"Almost everyday and twice on Sundays he likes to say," Joe said. "Sometimes when I'm having problems with my golf swing, I come out and watch him play a few holes. No matter what my problem is, watching him helps. If I'm having trouble with my timing, shoulder turn, or hand action, I like to come out and watch him. He doesn't have the full use of his legs so his swing is all about timing. It reminds me what can be achieved by mastering the simple things." Joe looked toward his two guests in the cart. "You understand?"

Chad nodded along with his father.

"Pretty good," Joe said. "Don't you think?"

"Awesome," Chad said. He felt inspired.

"Like I said, no matter what my problem is, watching him helps me," Joe said. "And here's a little secret: most of the times, my problems don't have anything to do with golf."

As they drove toward the clubhouse, Chad's dad said, "You ready for next year?"

"I will be by next month," Joe said. "You know there's a tour stop a couple of hours from here." He brought the golf cart to rest near the pro-shop. "Next summer, if you guys want to come out to the tournament, let me know and I'll get you tickets."

Joe Doaks was full of gifts.

age 12

"Of all the times you've been over here," Chad's mom said, carrying a bowl of popcorn into the room, "I can't believe this is the first time you've ever spent the night."

"Yep," Buzzy said, digging for a handful of buttery kernels.

Chad sat next to Buzzy on the floor. "Can we have ice cream after this?"

"Finish this first," his mom said. She returned to the sofa. "Where is your brother staying?"

"He was supposed to be spending the night over at a friend's house," Buzzy said. "But I saw a bunch of cars over in our driveway."

Chad turned to his mother. "Can we stay up to watch the late show?"

"If you want."

Buzzy stretched on the floor in front of the television. "This is much better than camping in the backyard." An hour later, sometime during the local news, he dozed off in the same position.

A nudge stirred him awake.

"Buzzy," Chad whispered.

Disoriented at first, Buzzy looked around the room. Theme music for the late show poured from the television. Once he

realized the surroundings, he sprang up. "I'm not asleep," he tried
to claim.

"I know," Chad said, "but it's time for bed anyway."

Buzzy followed Chad up the stairs.

"I hope the sleeping bag is okay," Chad said, pointing to it on
the floor near his bed.

"Sure." Buzzy unrolled it as Chad left the room. Before
unzipping the sleeping bag, Buzzy got an urge to use the
bathroom. He drifted toward the rectangular pattern of light
stamped on the hallway carpet. As he entered the open door, he
saw Chad standing over the sink brushing his teeth. "Oh," Buzzy
said, "tell me when you're done."

"Okay," Chad said through the swishing brush. He turned to
the mirror and continued brushing.

As Buzzy turned away, he noticed the pajama shorts Chad
wore. He could not help but glance toward the exposed legs. Since
the accident, almost two years before, Chad had kept the legs
hidden by long pants and flesh-covered garments. The shock of
the sight took Buzzy's breath. Coldness from the tile floor seeped
through his socks.

Buzzy stepped out into the hallway.

The blotchy red, pink, and peach patches of damaged skin took
root in Buzzy's mind. Parts of Chad's legs looked like an unstirred
bowl of tomato soup after someone poured in some milk. The
raised welts looked like someone had wrapped kite string around
both legs, cutting off the circulation. Splotches of healing skin
appeared shiny and fragile as tissue paper.

Buzzy envisioned jack-o-lanterns and the extraction of
pumpkin innards on *Halloween*. The smell and sight of the slimy
goop always turned his stomach. After seeing the scars, the same
queasiness came over him.

"All yours," Chad said after stopping in the doorway.

Buzzy tiptoed into the bathroom. After completing his
business, an idea came to him. He inspected the medicine cabinet
for a suitable prop. He tore a white tablet from a box of *Alka-
Seltzers* and placed it in his mouth. Once the tablet hit his saliva,

the fizzing foam built in his cheeks. He ran into to Chad's room barking like a dog. His mouth spewed a lathery froth. "Rurr, rurr, rurr," Buzzy snarled while twisting his head. Between foamy growls he announced, "Mad dog on the loose. Mad dog on the loose."

Chad fell onto his bed laughing.

Using a serious tone, Buzzy tried another joke. "I saw a raccoon in the woods today," he said through the white bubbles, "I went up to pet him on the head and he bit me."

Chad returned with, "Um, I think your mom just washed out your mouth with soap."

With a bubbly smile on his face, Buzzy snuck back to the bathroom. He wiped off his face, turned out the light, and slid into the sleeping bag.

Within a few minutes, things got quiet.

An orange nightlight glowed in the hallway.

Buzzy whispered, "Chad—." He searched for the right thing to say. He wanted to talk about the accident. He wanted to ask about the scars and if they hurt. He wanted to apologize. But, the words and nerve to deliver them escaped him. Instead, he came up with, "—whadda you wanna do tomorrow?"

"My dad's taking us to the par-3 course." After a few seconds, he added, "You wanna go, don't you?"

"Sure," Buzzy said and laid his head on the pillow. Visions of the scars held his mind hostage. Buzzy thought, *How could I keep forgetting what happened? Chad could never forget.* Buzzy swore he wouldn't either. He pledged to make up for the accident. Before slipping off to sleep, a tear escaped the corner of his eye, trailed down his temple, and soaked into the pillow.

* * *

"Thought you were gonna sleep all day," Buzzy said as Chad entered the kitchen.

"You been up awhile?"

"Not long," Buzzy said, working on a first bowl of cereal.

Chad looked over to his mother standing over the sink.

"I understand you guys made it past midnight," she said.

Chad pulled out a chair.

"Yep," Buzzy said. "I think Chad could've stayed up later, but I was too tired."

Chad shrugged his shoulders.

"Gonna be a good day for golf," Buzzy said.

Chad thought, *Is Buzzy always this chipper at breakfast? He's usually dragging himself to the bus stop.*

When they arrived at the par-3 course, Buzzy hopped from the backseat and stood waiting at the trunk. Once the trunk popped open, Buzzy reached in and grabbed the junior set of clubs. "I got these," he said before Chad had the chance.

Buzzy kept the clubs strapped to his shoulder as they headed for the first tee and only gave them up for Chad to carry on two holes. Whenever Buzzy yielded a turn carrying the bag, he tended the pin.

"Good shot," Buzzy said to Chad after almost every swing. When Chad sent a wayward shot toward some tall grass, Buzzy took off running, "I know exactly where it is." After a few seconds of searching, he pointed to the spot and yelled to Chad, "Here it is."

While they waited for greens to clear, Buzzy told jokes.

After Buzzy hit a bad shot, he smiled and asked for tips to improve.

Chad thought, *I knew Buzzy would like golf if he just gave it a chance.*

*   *   *

Chad sat at the breakfast table watching his dad scour the Saturday newspaper. "Um," Chad said. "I had a weird dream last night."

"Oh yeah," his dad said. The leafy pages rustled as he folded it. "Let's hear about it."

While waiting for the oven to do its work, Chad's mom propped her elbows on the island and looked in his direction.

"Okay. Okay. It's like this," Chad said, tugging at the tablecloth hem. "The dream starts out with me on the tee or something like that, and, I'm playing a dogleg par four. And I hit this humongous drive off the tee. And it's like as good as I can hit it. Okay? And, everyone on the tee agrees that I hit this great shot or something. And we all watch it make it around the corner. And, it should be right in the middle of the fairway in the perfect spot. Okay. And when we get up to where the ball should be, it's like, I can't find it."

"Okay," Chad's mom looked over to him and said. "Slow down a bit."

"Okay." Chad looked back and forth to both parents. "Everybody else in my group finds their ball and they keep playing toward the green. But, none of them hit their drives nearly as well as I did, but they all find their shots and keep playing. And they all think I'm in the middle of the fairway, so they're not even helping me find my ball. So I'm like wandering around in the middle of this fairway looking for my perfect drive and nobody's helping me find it. I keep thinking it should be right in the middle of the fairway. I also know this because the hole is familiar to me. It's like I've played it many times before.

"And to make matters worse, it's a hole that's next to a driving range. There are all these other balls in the fairway that came from the driving range and I have to check to see if each one belongs to me. So, in my dream, I'm out in this fairway thinking that every ball that I'm coming up to next is my perfect drive. But, each time I come up to one that I think is mine, it turns out to be just another ball from the driving range. And I can't find my ball anywhere. It's not where it should be. You know? It should be right in the middle of the fairway. I even start to look in areas that I know it couldn't be. And each time I look down, I find another range ball." Chad looked over to his mom.

She rubbed her hands in a dishrag and smiled.

"And worse still," Chad continued, "there's another group back on the tee waiting and watching. Then they start getting mad because I'm taking all this time looking for my perfect drive. And

I can't give up the search because it was a great shot and all. And it should be right in the middle of the fairway. And I've got this great round going, so I can't give up looking." Chad shrugged his shoulders. "That's all I can remember."

His dad grinned. "That's it?"

"Yeah, isn't it weird?"

"Weird?" his dad said, looking over to his mother. "Weird would be if golf balls were coming out of your ears and you went around picking 'em up and eating 'em."

"Come on Dad," Chad exhaled, exhausted from the explanation. "Don't you think it means something?"

"I think it means you made a hole-in-one," Chad's mom said. "Did you look in the hole?"

"It's a par-4," Chad said, setting his mother straight. "You can't make a hole-in-one on a par-4."

"Oh."

"Okay," his dad said, taking a more serious tone. "Come over here."

Chad rose and neared his father.

"I read something about this once," his dad said while reaching out with both hands. He messaged the temples of Chad's forehead. "It said that if you do this the morning after someone has a dream, you can actually tell them about their dream."

"Come on Dad."

"I'm serious," he said. He closed his eyes and rubbed. "Hold on here," he said as if making a discovery. "I think I'm getting something."

Chad stood still.

"It says here your dream means," he paused. "I can't quite make it out. It's still a little blurry."

Chad's mom scratched her head. "What could it be?"

"I got it!" His dad stopped the rubbing and opened his eyes. "Your dream means you want to be a dentist!"

"Oh, come on Dad."

*   *   *

Whenever the teacher prattled on, Chad played imaginary rounds of golf from his school desk. He rotated the yellow number-two pencil on a proper swing plane using the rubber eraser to launch wadded paper remnants from the spiraling wire of his notebook. A closed textbook served as the perfect teeing area for the pea-sized orbs aimed down the linoleum fairway lined by a forest of classmate shins. His slanted desktop provided a suitable putting surface guarded by a routed-groove pencil-holder hazard.

For Chad, the only thing more boring than classroom lectures were weekend sightseeing trips. At every roadside stop, he yawned at his parent's excitement for panoramic hillsides and bursts of colors from flowering trees. Winding through rocky mountain passes, they praised the adjacent stream trailing the road while Chad found looking at a magazine more interesting. Every landmark seemed the same.

Even a tram ride to the top of a mountain lacked excitement. They reached the mountaintop, disembarked the cab, and climbed steps to an observation deck already crowded with sightseers. As he looked across the valley below, Chad wondered how far he could drive a golf ball from the perched platform. He took aim at a pine tree that had outgrown its neighboring conifers. Not more than a hundred yards away, he imagined a well-hit drive flying over it. From the takeoff point, he pictured the dimpled white sphere sailing through the air against a cloudless blue sky with a trajectory easily carrying it above the noted pine tree. Next, Chad spotted a stream farther away. The foamy waters crashing and falling into a pile of rocks made the landmark significant against the darkness of shade. Chad imagined a golf ball zipping through the air like a bottle rocket. As much as he would have liked to include a smoke trail behind the golf ball, he decided against any such enhancement. The imaginary ball soared beyond the stream after curving slightly at the apex.

Chad began to discover intricacies in the scenery previously ignored. If standing at a high point, he estimated how high a golf shot would fly before dropping to the depths below. When looking up a hillside, he pictured the trajectory of a climbing shot and

guessed how much shorter it would travel. Dazzling colors of
leaves became apparent and served as a background for the make-
believe ball sailing through the air. Scents of flowering trees and
shrubs reached his nose. Babbling brooks and breezes whispered
in his ears. Different sun angles cast different lengths of shadows
depending on the time of day. Clouds occasionally blocked the
sunshine and sped along the earth's surface.

Occasionally, the imaginary golf ball casts its smaller shadow
as it chased patches of shade as if it they were moving putting
greens. At dusk, golf balls flew through the air like shooting stars.

Chad imagined a flight pattern reflective of the perfect swing.
The arcs, distance, and spin never flew along unrealistic or
cartoonish paths. There were no loop-d-loops, no corkscrewing
spirals, and no mid-air stops with abrupt changes of direction. Any
enhancements beyond reality depreciated the vision.

As an adult, Chad continued to imagine. Whenever the earth
rose around him or dropped in front of him, his mind wandered to
the flight of a golf ball. He knew to never aim for water, but
whenever he stood next to the ocean or a tranquil lake, a long
drive came to mind. It did not have to be a natural landmark.
When he visited New York City, he rode through the canyon of
heroes in lower Manhattan and launched an imaginary mid-iron
straight down Broadway without ever veering near the sidewalks
of people making up the rough. He looked through the telescope
from atop the Empire State Building and thought of a golf ball
flying toward the round circular roof of Madison Square Garden.
Similar daydreams played on the Grand Canyon rim, below Mt.
Rushmore, and around the Grand Tetons.

To make the fantasy golf ball fly along a perfect path, Chad
inevitably concentrated on the perfect swing. Unable to control the
urge atop the mountain sightseeing perch, he lined his feet, hips,
and shoulders while flexing his knees. With both parents glancing
over, he took imaginary swings propelling the inaugural launches.
Chad stared into the distance tracking the flight.

He had discovered a means of transforming the mundane to magnificent. After a few more swings, he smiled in the direction of his parents and said, "Where we going next?"

* * *

"And if one goes into the crowd," Chad explained to Buzzy, "it's not like a foul ball. You can't keep it." Chad felt responsible and hoped to avoid possible embarrassment. With each passing mile, he decided to furnish a list of last-minute reminders. "If one comes near you, stay clear of it. Don't even touch it."

Buzzy lifted his head from the passenger-side door and nodded.

Chad sat wide-eyed absorbing the passing scenery. The excitement kept sleep away for much of the night before. As the silent miles passed, he glanced over to see that Buzzy had fallen asleep. His hair rubbed against the glass window and his mouth fell open. Chad decided to let him rest.

After seeing the first sign for the tournament, Chad grabbed the headrest and pointed. "There it is." He sank back and nudged Buzzy.

Buzzy opened his eyes and smacked his lips.

After finding a parking space in a remote lot, they locked the doors and hurried to the nearest shuttle bus stop. As they waited for a ride to the main gate, Chad's dad handed each of them a colored cardboard ticket with a loop of string attached. "Wrap it here," he said. "Like this." Chad watched as he slipped the string around a front belt loop and slid the rectangular ticket through it.

Chad pointed at a group of people approaching the waiting area. "See," he said to Buzzy, "everyone wears 'em like that."

As the tickets fluttered at waist high in the breeze, Buzzy said, "It looks like they all got a teabag in their pocket."

Within minutes, an open-air shuttle arrived and they hopped aboard. After making a few more stops, the bus traveled across a few side streets and terminated at the main gate. Riders exited by sliding to one side while the driver announced the shuttle made a return trip to the same spot every fifteen minutes.

As they entered the main gate, Chad swallowed in the surroundings. Hundreds of metal rods surrounded each hole. Similar to steel rebar, the rods had their tops twisted so they curled like a pig's tail. Like a dispatched army separating spectators from contestants, the bars stood at attention holding miles of sagging yellow rope in the coiled loops. The dangling waist-high barrier upheld crowd control effectively as razor wire. Concession stands with wheels and trailer hitches camped in strategic spots for any patrons overcome with hunger or thirst. Portable toilets hid behind leafy branches and mulched swales. Near the 18th green, a large permanent leader board, freshened with a new coat of paint, stood ready to hold the changing names of players along with green and red numbers to report their relation to par. Smaller scoreboards in remote areas provided updates on the leaders and approaching players. Erected for advantageous viewing, grandstands of various capacities rose from hillsides. Depending on one's credentials, seating arrangements varied from a grassy hillside to cushioned folding chairs. Excavation of land and extermination of grass were uninvited consequences of the temporary structures with assurances granted that rebirth would occur within weeks of their removal. Tarpaulins covered lower parts of the erected engineering to hide the scars. A pair of carved wooden figures depicting a sponsor trademark stood alone in the teeing areas. On the greens, new flags fluttered in the breeze. A bluish-green dye circulated in the lakes and streams to convince any doubters the hazards contained real water.

As the crowds flowed through the main gate, Chad envisioned an army of volunteers that ensured the smooth operation. A cleaning brigade swept through to service garbage bins by trading plastic bags full of trash with empty ones. A brigade of mowers left crisscross patterns on the fairways and greens. The contestants, groomed and equipped, advanced across the checkerboard pattern like knights, bishops, and kings.

"Pairing sheets." A volunteer stood inside the gate holding a stack of papers. He repeated loud enough to draw attention. "Get your pairing sheets here."

Chad's dad pointed. "Grab us a couple of those."

Chad practically mugged the guy.

"I already know Joe's tee time," his dad said, scanning the sheet, "but this will let us know who might be in front or behind his group." He flipped it over to find a course layout. "He should be about on the sixth hole by now. Why don't we go catch his group and follow him in?"

They all agreed.

He pointed to the side of a rope-lined fairway and said, "This way."

*　*　*

Chad's nerves tingled. While they waited at a crosswalk, he grabbed the yellow nylon rope and shook it. When the fairway cleared, a volunteer dropped the line allowing spectators a chance to traverse the playing grounds. Like worn carpet in front of a doorway, a week's worth of heavy foot traffic wore the checkerboard-patterned grass to a light brown.

They crossed several fairways and made their way around other tees and greens. Along the way, Chad stopped to watch players execute shots. He applauded with the crowds after good shots and roared for great ones. "Dad . . . Dad . . . Dad—," he urged the attention of his father. "Look, who that is. He's, like, my favorite player." Chad spotted another player on an adjacent tee. He swiveled his head from player to his father. "Dad . . . Dad . . . Dad—," he said, making sure his dad did not miss anything. "Look who that is."

His dad repeated the same response. "Just slow down a bit."

Great golf shots awed Chad. "Dad . . . Dad . . . Dad—," he ached to share the delight, "—did you see that shot?"

He longed to be everywhere on the golf course at the same time.

Several times, his dad motioned for calm with his hands. "Slow down, now."

Chad tried to control his excitement, but found it difficult. Even for the simple questions. "Dad . . . Dad . . . Dad . . . can me and Buzzy go up there and watch that group tee off?"

"Yes," his father said. "Just stay close enough that I can see you."

Compared to television, Chad discovered the benefits of watching in-person. He endured the heat with the players and marched every step of more than five miles with them. Perspiration staining his shirt matched those of the players and caddies. Geometry lessons applied to the heights of trees and hills, the depths of valleys, and the undulations of multi-tiered putting greens. Chad learned how early the contestants arrived at the course, how long they warmed-up, how long the round took, how long some players mixed with the media, and how long others practiced after their round. Compared to television coverage, Chad learned he could spend a whole day as a spectator at a tournament and catch only a small portion.

At the tournament, Chad became an exemplary student. He took mental notes of how different players approached each shot. Golf at the professional level hardly compared to the recreational version. By watching a good player, Chad figured he could improve. Solid golf shots collided perfectly in the middle of the clubface. Divots flew from fairways like green hairpieces. Shots escaped bunkers after clubheads thumped lightly in the sand. Chad itched to get on the course and imitate the action.

Chad bonded with the throngs of spectators. They all wanted to bear witness to something great. Thousands of people remained quiet enough for an operating room surgeon and erupted with roaring explosions after witnessing a miracle. On a bet, these same people would not extend two feet in front of their usual playing partners. But at the tournament, they had complete trust in the professionals to stand so close to the line of fire.

Chad decided to join the brave bystanders at the front of a tee. He leaned over the ropes, down a narrow slice of mowed turf stretching about fifty yards. Across the narrow strip, other spectators looked backwards as if standing on a platform waiting for the next arriving train. Chad watched a player take a swing and heard the familiar *'crack'* of solid contact. He followed the forthcoming ball through the air. Just like a bullet train, he heard the high-pitched whistling of the golf ball cutting through the air: *sssssssssSSSSSUUUUUuuuuu*. As it passed, the whistling dimples dropped a lower octave. It happened all in a flash, but he heard the ball cutting through the air. Mesmerized, Chad stayed in the same spot to watch two different groups tee off.

*   *   *

Security at the golf tournament interested Buzzy. From the time he passed through the entrance, he scoured the grounds for gate crashing opportunities. Unlike the giant walls and towering fences preventing invasions at stadiums and ballparks, he believed sneaking into a golf tournament would be a snap. Breaches were everywhere in the forms of paths emerging from wooded areas and gaps in hedgerows.

Beyond perimeter surveillance, Buzzy became fascinated with those working at the tournament. Hardhats worn by the volunteers at fairway crosswalks made them look as if they came from construction jobs. Marshals around the greens and tees raised slender signs demanding silence from the crowd when players required concentration. Local Boy Scout troops toted small scoreboards with every group. Over the top of their uniforms, they wore the same cotton shoulder strap with a waist-high cup that normally hoisted flags over long parade routes. Buzzy figured the carrying part was simple and supposed he could do the job as long as someone else told him when to change the numbers. He liked the privileged aspect of being inside the ropes. Only problem was, Buzzy didn't want to be a Boy Scout.

Buzzy liked darting through the crowds. The crack of the golf ball sounded like the firing of a starter's pistol. Each time he heard it, Buzzy sprinted to the next spot hoping to be first. When the ropes dropped at the crosswalks, it was like the gate opening for a racehorse. Buzzy dashed down the fairway and waited for the crowds to catch him. Often he took a step outside the marked boundary to lean over and touch the grass. "Feel how smooth this is," he said to Chad as he rubbed the surface. "It's just like carpet." Buzzy broke off a few short blades.

"Um, these fairways are like the putting greens on the par-3 course," Chad said.

"Let's go boys," Chad's dad said, exiting the crosswalk.

Buzzy spat. Being outdoors awoke a need to expel some saliva. Most times, the small amount of white foam he sprayed helped rid his mouth of a bad taste. It also made him feel older. He often took requests on the school playground performing tricks that included a stream between his two front teeth like a squirt gun. The real showstopper involved the expulsion of mucous in a long slimy string dangling from his lips. Before the hanging hocker hit the point of no return, Buzzy sucked the slimy string back into his mouth as if it were a yo-yo. Drinking milk beforehand aided the required consistency for the grand finale. Wayne taught him that one.

By the first hour, Buzzy had seen everything. The heat and boredom wore him down. No longer interested in sprints from the starting gate, he slowed the pace to a meandering in the shade.

Chad continued at high speed. "Isn't this awesome?" He must have asked Buzzy the same question a dozen times all day. It started to bug him. "Watch this shot," Chad would also repeat. But they all looked the same to Buzzy. All day Chad introduced players. "That's So-and-So," and provided a little background information like, "he won The Masters."

But it remained uninteresting to Buzzy.

Just as he grew tired of the heat, Buzzy grew tired of Chad's colorful comments. When Chad provided an impromptu introduction, Buzzy responded with a nonchalant, "I never heard-a-him."

"See that guy?" Chad said, "That's So-and-So, and he's the rookie that almost won last week."

Buzzy spat on the ground and gave the same response. "I never heard-a-him."

The lackadaisical attitude appeared to frustrate Chad. With disbelief on his face, he repeated the question. "Um, you really never heard of him?"

It became entertaining for Buzzy. Even if he knew a player, he still responded, "I never heard-a-him."

* * *

Chad saw his dad waving at the tenth tee.

"I think that's Joe's group," his dad said in a hushed voice. "Don't be disappointed if he doesn't see you. And don't try to get his attention. Remember, he's at work."

"Um, okay," said Chad and took off toward the green.

Joe Doaks completed the tenth hole with a tap-in par. Chad and Buzzy scurried to a spot behind the next tee. By the time they raced down the next fairway, Chad's dad already stood holding a spot.

En route to his ball in the fairway, Joe veered close to the crowd. "Hey fellas," he said with a wave and a smile.

Even though his dad explained the possibility of not being able to talk with Joe at all, Chad appreciated the fact he acknowledged their presence. He only hoped it had not been a distraction.

They followed Joe the rest of the way clapping for every good shot and sharing nervous tension when he got in a tight spot. In awe, they watched as he calculated and executed a hook shot that wrapped around a tree and landed on the green. He climbed to the putting surface, read the correct break from fifteen-feet, and curled it into the cup for a birdie. On the next hole, they watched his iron shot from the fairway. Wet dirt, grass, and roots exploded from the ground as if someone stuck a firecracker into a wormhole. The diamond-hard golf ball flew high in the air and landed soft as melting ice cream.

As they approached the eighteenth fairway, several canvas tents, large enough to hold a three-ring-circus, caught Chad's attention. Instead of watching the final putt, he asked for permission to explore the monstrous midway.

Under the big top, Chad strolled grassy aisles while peering at exhibits that displayed the latest golf gadgets. Booths offered video swing analysis and indoor driving ranges. A remote pro-shop rang up sales of hats, shirts, windbreakers and any other golfing merchandise containing enough space to stitch or stamp the host country club and tournament logo.

Chad noticed a booth promoting a nearby golf camp. The display contained illuminated posters depicting the golf course and a lodge that housed campers. Chad stared at the photos and imaged himself as one of the kids receiving instructions. He grabbed a brochure.

As they exited the tent, Chad saw his dad waiting under the shade of a nearby tree. Unable to contain his excitement, he jogged over and presented the flyer. "Dad . . . Dad . . . Dad—," he panted for air, "—check this out."

His dad opened the tri-fold pamphlet. "Looks interesting."

Chad fidgeted with excitement. "Can I go next year?"

"Maybe," his dad shrugged his shoulders and nodded. "We'll talk about it later."

Chad twisted his torso and clinched his fist as if he sank a long putt. "Yes!" The initial favorable reaction called for celebration.

*   *   *

Joe Doaks emerged from the scorer's trailer and headed for the practice range. On the way, he shook hands and signed autographs. They followed behind and joined a sparse crowd of spectators sitting in aluminum stands at the driving range. They talked about how the range balls used by pros appeared brand new and craved a bagful of their own. Caddies grabbed balls off a pyramid-shaped stack and tossed them to their player. Every swing from every player appeared flawless. Instead of a range picker circling in the dust, the pros hit to flagsticks and raised greens on a tidy range mowed with crisscross patterns like the faultless fairways.

"No rubber tees and mats for these guys," said Chad's dad.

After hitting a handful of shots, Joe slid his club into the upright golf bag. He gave his caddy some instructions and made his way toward the spectators. He stopped first to talk with apparent members of his family and then lifted the yellow security rope. A few waiting kids stuck golf caps and pens in front of him hoping he would add his signature. After autographing the last hat, he reached to shake hands with Chad's dad. "*Stretch*," the touring pro said. "How've you been?"

"Great," Chad's dad said with a smile. "Nice round today."

"Thanks," said Joe, "but it coulda been better." He stuck out a hand to Chad. "And how's *Stretch, Jr.?*"

"Um, great Mr. Doaks," Chad said, smiling while shaking hands. "I'd like you to, um, meet my friend, Buzzy." He pointed to Buzzy standing next to him.

Joe extended his hand once more to Buzzy. "Hello Buzzy."

"Hi ya Joe," Buzzy spit on the ground and repeated the same line posed all day, "How come I never heard of you?"

"You never heard of me?" Joe didn't appear rattled by the comment. "Maybe you haven't been listening."

"Don't worry Mr. Doaks," Chad said somewhat embarrassed. "He hadn't heard of anybody."

Chad's dad stretched the side of his mouth and said in a low voice, "Neighbor's kid."

*   *   *

For the first thirty minutes in the car, the boys remained excited and full of energy. Although they hadn't moved far in traffic, both Chad and Buzzy lobbed comments back and forth in the backseat recalling the day's highlights.

"You know," Buzzy said, "I saw other people wearing T-shirts out there."

Chad's dad looked in the rear view mirror with a funny face. "You did?"

"Yeah," said Buzzy, "and you told me they wouldn't let 'em in."

"Well," he said, "Like I said, better safe than sorry." A few minutes passed and he changed the subject. "Well boys," he said, "what was your favorite part of the day?"

"Um, um, um," Chad muttered while his brain needed time to find a highlight. "I liked everything."

Buzzy provided more insight. "I liked those guys holding up the signs that told everybody to shut up. If it were up to me, I'd smack people in the head with that paddle."

Everyone grinned.

As the miles rolled on the odometer, the hum of rubber tires on the road droned them to silence. Chad gazed out the window and predicted the time between mile markers. About halfway home, he spoke again. "You know what?"

His dad looked to him through the rearview mirror. "What?"

"Someday, I'm like, gonna play in that tournament."

"Keep practicing," his dad said. "And you never know."

Next, Buzzy made his announcement. "You know what?"

Chad's dad took the bait again. "What?"

"Someday," Buzzy said, "I'm gonna be a marshal at that tournament."

*   *   *

"Okay class," the seventh grade teacher announced, "your first writing assignment will be a two hundred word essay about your favorite day last summer."

A few students smiled and sat higher while others moaned and dropped their heads atop crossed arms.

"I know that you've probably had to do this before," she continued. "But I think it's a good way to get you back in the habit of writing and it gives me a chance to get to know you a little better."

A hand went up.

She pointed to Buzzy. "Yes Buzzy."

Buzzy looked around the room as if he wanted to make sure everyone heard his voice. "Does it have to be exactly two hundred words?"

"Not exactly," she said. "But it should be at least two hundred words."

Chad rarely asked questions in class, but decided to get some clarification on the assignment.

"Yes Chad," the teacher said, pointing in his direction.

"What if, like, two of us, like, write about the same thing?"

"That's no problem," she said, "just pick your favorite day and tell me about it."

Chad worked a few nights on the paper and submitted it on Friday:

I played in my very first golf tournament last summer. What made it even more special was the fact that I shot my best score in golf while playing in the Schoolboy Junior golf tournament. The tournament was played at the short hills municipal course and there were alot of other kids playing in the tournament. Most of them were older. I was a little nervous about playing in a tournament all by myself, but I knew all my practicing would payoff. My mom and dad kept telling me it was most important to have fun and relax and they were right. They both came and wached me play. It was hot and we all got a sun burn. When I stepped up to a shot, I just thought about having fun and relaxing. I made a 20 foot putt for a par on the 2nd hole. It was almost good enough to win a trophy. There were alot of other kids in my age group. I can't wait until next summer to play in the Schoolboy tournament again and be in the same age group. It was my best day of the year because it was the best round of my life and it came at the best time. When it counted.

On Monday, the teacher returned the assignments. Chad noticed a few corrections in red pencil and the assigned letter grade of 'B' at the top of the paper. The teacher included a handwritten note that said, *'Congratulations!'*

Buzzy almost forgot what he slapped together late Thursday night. He could guarantee one thing; he had met the word-count requirement. When returned, he found that every sentence of his essay appeared to demand attention from the teacher's red pencil. The besmirched composition earned a 'C-minus'. The teacher's written comment was *'Sounds like fun'*. Buzzy read over it again:

My Favorite Day Of Last Summer
by Buzzy Odom

My favorite day of last summer was when Wayne took me to go fishing. It was my favorite day because I like to go fishing and I like my older brother Wayne. We went to Coleman lake with a canoo from Waynes buddy and we tide it to the top of the car it was red. We took the canoo off the top of the car and put it into the lake. My brother let me sit in the front of the canoo and he sat in the back of the canoo. We paddle around the lake looking for honey holes. My fishing pole worked real good. My brother got mad when I made a noise and I scaird away the fish and cussed me out. We caught some bass and brim and croppy and one cat fish. My brother showed me how to clean guts out of fish and put them in the freezer. My brother was nice to take me fishing accept when he pushed me in the lake. That is why my favorite day of last summer was the day that my brother took me to go fishing.

Buzzy stared at the grade for a while. He believed he deserved a higher mark. *I ought to have gotten credit for creativity,* Buzzy thought. *Maybe I should've provided more information.*

I should've told the truth.

Wayne never took me fishing.

age 13

Chad's mom continued to fret all the way up to check-in. "You know C.J.," she said, observing other campers in line. "You can call anytime, day or night, and we'll come get you."

"Um, Mom," Chad said, rolling his eyes.

"You don't even need an excuse," she said, "if you want to come home."

"I'll be fine. It's gonna be fun."

"I know, but just in case, you know you can call."

Chad changed the subject. "Look at Buzzy's suitcase."

Buzzy held up a half-filled school duffle bag. "I like to travel light."

Undeterred, Chad's mom continued, "Make sure you write us a post card. Make sure you eat well." A few seconds later she whispered to Chad, "Make sure you put your dirty clothes in the plastic bag." As they neared the table she said, "You know you can call anytime."

Chad grew tired of all the reminders. The nagging started to sound the same. He nodded each time hoping to appease her.

After signing-in, they joined a handful of others for a quick tour. The main hall, a two-story building planted on the side of a hill, featured a large open space suitable for presentations and seminars. An idle ping-pong table sat on one side of the room and folded chairs stood in a wheeled rack on the other. A floor below contained the cafeteria filled with round tables and a kitchen equipped with stainless steel fixtures.

"Diners enjoy looking out to the forest," the counselor giving the tour said, "but truck drivers hate to walk down the stairs to make deliveries." Adjacent to the main hall stood the three-story, rectangular sleeping lodge secluded in a tower of trees. "Right this way," said the camp counselor leading the group under a covered walkway and up a flight of stairs. As the group arrived on the third floor, he continued, "Campers will bunk on the second and third floors. Camp counselors are housed in separate rooms on the first floor."

Chad first noticed the exposed wooden rafters supporting a vaulted ceiling. Rotating blades on suspended fans stirred the air. Half-walls partitioned areas for two sets of bunk beds with a pair of cabinets guarding each entrance. Pipes from the sprinkler system ran through the roof rafters and a sign on the wall designated the building as a non-smoking facility.

Chad's mom pointed to the sign. "If you boys see anyone smoking, please report it."

A narrow hallway separated the sleeping quarters from a restroom large enough to accommodate crowds. A community shower loomed behind a wall lined with sinks and accompanying mirrors. The smell of fresh paint adorned dented stalls partitioning toilets.

"There'll be a brief presentation back at the main hall in fifteen minutes," said the counselor. "Parents are invited if you want to stick around." The counselor checked a clipboard and pointed to the cubicle near the door. "You two," he said to Chad and Buzzy, "take this bunk." He continued down the aisle with the clipboard assigning campers to available spaces.

"I got top," Buzzy said.

Chad's first urge was to argue for the spot. Instead, he shrugged his shoulders.

"Drop your golf clubs up by the school bus," the counselor said loud enough for everyone in the sleeping quarters to hear. "We'll be hitting the course this afternoon."

Chad's parents stayed for the orientation program. The director of golf camp introduced the counselors, distributed a facilities map, and dictated a list of rules. Next, he discussed the schedule for the week's activities and presented a slideshow about past years at camp.

Chad looked over to his mom and noticed a familiar worry on her face. At the conclusion of the presentation, she gave him a hug and kissed him on the forehead. "Call us if you need anything," she said one last time.

She even hugged Buzzy.

Before retreating to the car, she offered one last piece of concern. "Please be careful."

*   *   *

"The bus leaves for the course in five minutes," announced the camp director. He dispatched a group of counselors around the lodge to circulate the message.

With no time to unpack, Chad headed for the parking lot and climbed through the swinging bus doors.

Buzzy followed behind and sat next to him.

One counselor lifted golf bags through a rear door while the other stacked them in the last rows. Once everyone found a seat and the headcount matched the roster, the front doors swung closed.

A small fan attached above the driver's sun visor was all the air conditioning available, so most of the square window panes remained lowered. As the bus spewed exhaust, Chad stared out the window and discovered other park amenities. Conversations reacquainting friends from previous years at camp surrounded him. Once the golf course came into view, the level of anticipation rose. Glimpses of tees and greens were only available until the final turn into the entrance road. From that point, an unobstructed view of the entire length of two holes stretched alongside. Like alerted wading birds, golfers already on the course looked up when they heard the rumbling school bus approach. As it reached the practice putting green, the bus let out one last belch. The driver locked the brakes and swung the door handle open.

A counselor scurried toward the rear to help unload the golf bags while another stayed near the front to direct those exiting the bus. He repeated the same thing several times. "Grab your 5-iron and head down to the range." He pointed to an area under a large tree. "Leave your bags over there for now." Chad heard him announce to the next bunch stepping off. "Grab your 5-iron. Leave your bags over there."

The unsheathing of iron clubs from bags created a rattling sound. Chad joined the stream of armed golfers making their way to the driving range.

Other counselors stood waiting for them on the lowest platform of the three-tiered practice tee. "Go ahead and take a seat," said one of them pointing to a grassy slope.

Mr. Bob Brown, the same person that gave the welcoming speech at the lodge, took center stage. "Okay boys," he said to the crowd, "let's get started."

Out in the sun, Mr. Brown looked like a real golf professional. Even though slightly rotund and balding, most of the physical flaws hid behind a pressed golf shirt and creased long pants. A darker shade tanned his face and arms, and because he wore a hat, his forehead and bare dome faded to the same pale hue that matched other parts of his body protected from the sun's rays.

"My name is Mr. Brown," he addressed the crowd. "You can call me Mr. Brown or Mr. Bob. Some of you may hear other counselors call me *Chief* or other things, like *Ground-round* Bob Brown because of my many recipes using hamburger."

An older camper sitting next to Chad whispered from the side of his mouth. "What they really call him is *Round* Bob Brown."

"I've even been called Bob *Brown and Serve*, again because of my many talents in the kitchen," the director continued. "But you campers should address me as Mr. Brown."

Chad looked up to the older camper sitting next to him and smiled.

"I see a few familiar faces out there," *Round* Bob Brown continued while pointing over the crowd. "How many of you were here last year? Raise your hand." He recognized a familiar face in the crowd and said while pointing, "Hey guy."

During the week, Chad learned *Round* Bob Brown found it difficult to remember names and often hung a generic *'Guy'* on everyone. Commonly heard phrases during golf camp from *Round* Bob Brown: *"Hey guy. How's the family?"* and, *"Nice shot guy,"* and, *"Hey guy, keep it down over there."* If required, he sometimes added a descriptor. He used *Big Guy* when referring to both gentle giants and the smallest of campers. *Wise Guy* or *Smart Guy* usually illustrated his displeasure with an individual and *Tough Guy* deflated anyone feeling rambunctious.

Chad noticed a large number of campers with their hands raised in response to his question.

Round Bob Brown took a silent count. "That's about half of you. Well, welcome back. Now, for those new campers, we also want to welcome you to what we hope will be a fun week and a week in which you will improve your golf game. We like to start off with what we'll call our initial analysis of your skills. What we do here is a lot like following a recipe."

Some in the crowd moaned.

"Each of your instructors here on the range will be like a chef," said *Round* Bob Brown. "They all have a special recipe for success in golf. The great tasting dinner they're preparing includes all the ingredients for you to become a better golfer. For those of you that were here last year, do you remember what you are?"

A few campers raised their hands.

"You there, guy." *Round* Bob Brown pointed to the closest kid. "What are you?"

"We're a full-course meal," the kid said loud enough to be heard by those closest to him.

"That's right," said *Round* Bob Brown. "You're a four-course meal. Your golf game will be just like a dining experience and it's up to our chefs here to prepare you properly."

Chad sniffed the air for aromas.

"For those of you that don't know," said *Round* Bob Brown rubbing at his belly, "I enjoy cooking. Instead of classifying golfers based on a number or letter system, I've come up with my own system here at camp. Now, we all know there are all kinds of different types of ovens. Any of you seen a microwave before? Well, in a microwave, you pop in a prepackaged meal, press a few buttons, and within minutes, the whole thing's done. It's nice and neat. Some of you boys will fit into the Microwave group.

"Now you also have Hot Plates, Toaster Ovens, Barbecue Grills, Conventional Ovens and Crockpots," *Round* Bob Brown said. "You guys know what a Crockpot is? A Crockpot takes time to get the job done. You start early preparing all the ingredients. You add them one at a time and let them simmer at a low heat. The meal cooks all day. This type of cooking takes a lot of time and requires a lot of cleaning up afterward. Some of you boys will be in the Crockpot group."

Next to Chad, the older boy murmured, "Sounds like a crock of you-know-what."

Chad looked over and smiled again.

Round Bob Brown provided a similar description for every culinary grouping. Despite the groans and snide whispers circulating through the audience, he reached the end of the list. "Then you have Conventional Ovens, like the ones in most of your homes. And they fall somewhere in-between Microwaves and Crockpots. Some of you boys will be Conventional Ovens and we'll group you accordingly. Don't worry too much about what group you're put in, just remember our main goal is to make that perfect recipe that will improve your golf game. Now, any questions?"

Someone spoke up, "What happens if the meal gets burned?"

Laughter erupted.

"Did it take you a whole year to come up with that one wise guy? Did you think you signed up for a cooking class?" *Round* Bob Brown smiled as if he enjoyed the banter. "I'll tell you what we have for that. What we have for that is sunscreen."

"What about popcorn?" another kid said. "You can't make popcorn in a Crockpot."

"You're about as sharp as a marble, aren't you smart guy?" After a short pause, *Round* Bob Brown said, "Just to let any other of you wise guys know, we also have a category called Campfire. The campfire is the most basic of cooking means. You've all roasted marshmallows and hot dogs on sticks. That's about all you can cook on a campfire. They're a primitive stove; not very useful. Now we've been doing this golf camp for five years now, and just to let you know, we've not seen one golfer worthy of the Campfire group. But, if we get enough wise guys like you all, we may just be able to start one."

A few nervous smiles joined additional moans and groans.

Round Bob Brown looked up from his clipboard and smiled. "Okay, break into groups of ten for each instructor and take a few shots with your 5-iron."

*   *   *

Chad joined Buzzy and a small group sitting on a hillside. The first name was called and a nearby kid stood and approached the pile of range balls.

"Okay," the instructor said, "you'll each have a chance to hit three shots. Don't worry about the clipboard; I'm just here to take a few notes."

Buzzy massaged the turf at his side and plucked blades of grass with both hands.

Chad grew nervous.

After the first kid completed his turn, the instructor said, "Next up, Buzzy Odom."

Buzzy pulled a tee from his pocket and drove it in the ground with the end of his 5-iron like a carpenter with a hammer. He placed a range ball on top. The miniature pedestal suspended the ball in mid-air floating it free from the trappings of terra firma. Buzzy swiveled his hips and knees as if he were trying to keep an invisible hula-hoop afloat. He waggled his club in crazy circles behind the ball until he accidentally knocked it off the peg.

Chad had seen the act before. It appeared Buzzy brought the show on the road.

Buzzy said to the instructor, "Does that count?"

None of the onlookers laughed.

After completing his set of mediocre golf shots, Buzzy turned to the instructor and stroked the air with a pointer finger. "Mark me down as a Crockpot."

"Okay," said the instructor confirming Buzzy's assessment. "You're with the Crockpots. Next up, Chad Ashworth."

Chad felt the eyes of strangers upon him as he rose from the hill. He lumbered toward the stack of range balls. Unlike Buzzy, he wanted to prove his proficiency by playing it from the sod. Although brave, he later wished he had taken advantage of a tee. Chad grew nervous and anxious like a getaway driver in the movies waiting for a tardy accomplice. His heart raced and breathing became difficult.

On his first swing, Chad took a proper grip and stance, but he darted the club back too fast. Wanting to get some extra distance, he used more effort at the top than usual. As the clubhead approached the ball, the angle swooped too steep and it dove into the turf with a loud thud before ever reaching the golf ball. The ideal swing plane crashed.

As Chad pulled the plugged club from the mud, he felt the embarrassment of a scrubbed launch.

Humiliation followed.

"Don't worry," said the instructor. "Give it another shot."

Chad had no escape hatch. Flecks of mud splattered the marooned range ball. He mustered a bit of courage for a second swing and hoped the instructor allowed one miscue. As the clubhead uncoiled on the second try, it failed to meet the ball on the sweet spot. In fact, the connection landed far out on the toe squirting the ball into a wooded area lining the driving range. Shoddy contact on the clubface traveled up the shaft and stung his hands.

Chad shook his head in disgust. He wanted to look back to his dad in the aluminum lawn chair for advice, but realized he would not be there.

"One more try," said the instructor. "Make it a good one."

Although the third shot improved, it still fell short of his potential.

The instructor made some notes on his clipboard. "Okay big guy," he said and then called for the next camper.

Suffocating with disappointment, Chad found it hard to breath. He wanted to shrink into the blades of grass on the hill. His head slumped between his knees. He hated golf and wanted to give it up forever.

As the groups were announced, Chad found himself with the worst golfers in camp, the Crockpots.

A pair of golf shoes worn by the evaluator approached him. "We know you're better than this group," the instructor said in a low voice. "But we thought you probably wanted to be in the same group as your friend Buzzy."

Chad felt no consolation. He remained silent as they rode back to the lodge. He pondered leaving camp. Even though his parents just dropped him off, he knew they would come and get him. *How could he be so bad? How could he ever play golf again? How could he stay a whole week?*

As the school bus came to a halt, the driver made an announcement. "Dinner will be served in the main hall in thirty minutes."

Chad lagged behind other campers filing off the bus. When he reached the sleeping quarters, he and Buzzy met the other campers sharing the bunk space. Introductions were brief as the two boys hurried off to play ping-pong.

Buzzy wandered to the bathroom.

Chad decided to unpack his luggage. As he unzipped it, he found a note on top of his folded clothes. It said:

C.J. –

*Have a great time at camp. Here are some post cards &
stamps for you to write when you get a chance. Let us know
how you are doing and that you're okay. Have a great time
and remember to call anytime if you need us. Please be
careful.*

   We both love you very much.
   Mom & Dad

Chad's face became flush. No one else appeared to see him, so he folded the letter and tucked it under a stack of shirts.

Notions of quitting golf lingered in Chad's mind. Throughout dinner and the evening program, he rarely spoke a word. A terrible afternoon on the practice range had him thinking he should never play golf again. Lying in the bottom bunk after lights out, he dwelt on the horrible driving range performance: *How could he ever face the group of kids that saw him flub so many shots during the evaluation? How much fun could he really have being stuck with the Crockpots? Why keep playing a game in which he obviously stunk? Why was he so nervous? Maybe he was always bad at golf and just didn't know it. Why not quit?*

Just before dosing off, he remembered how his mother encouraged golf. She decorated every year with a golf theme on his birthday. She might be disappointed if he quit, but she would understand. She even said he could come home anytime he wanted. He recalled the countless hours spent hitting golf balls with his dad. He remembered how he always tried to help and always cheered him up after a bad shot. If he gave up golf, he hoped his dad would get over it. He even remembered what Joe Doaks said about what others thought. But, that didn't help much either.

Finally, he fell asleep.

*   *   *

As he dressed the next morning, Chad forced a smile. He decided that if things didn't improve, he'd have no problem making the call and going home. At breakfast, he remained quiet. On the school bus, he grabbed a window seat. As the bus sputtered toward the golf course, he leaned his head against the cool glass and looked out. A family rode bicycles along a path and an old man fished from a pier that extended into a lake.

Once the golf course came into view, Chad started to feel different. What moved him was so simple, yet so complex. He sat up and pressed against the window. The sun, still below the visible horizon, stamped the sod with spiky silhouettes of treetops like pointy tops of a crown. Shafts of bright light poured through slits in the forest igniting the rolling hills of the fairway like spotlights on a stage. Chad felt a yearning to be on that stage.

Ahead on the putting green, a striped pin stood at attention in the morning breeze. The flagstick, rising from the middle, looked like a giant arrow that hit the bulls-eye. Chad craved a chance to take aim.

A misting of dew covered the green carpet as if someone had squeezed a giant spray bottle. Footprints and mowers had not blemished the surface. Chad ached to be the first to make a mark.

White stakes stood near the roadway defining the boundaries in which competition took place. Refueled by the sights, Chad desired to be in the arena. Small bushes on both sides of the roadside fairway indicated a distance of 150 yards to the green. Chad longed to get home from there. As the bus passed the next teeing area, Chad noticed the colored markers at five different locations and realized how golf made allowances for everyone. Golf made allowances for him.

One disastrous day could not crush his enthusiasm. A few bad swings would not cancel his dreams.

He would prove the evaluators wrong.

He would prove himself wrong.

*   *   *

Campers didn't need a posted schedule or wristwatches to determine free time. All they had to do was listen for the *chick-chack* of the ping-pong ball echoing from the main hall: *chick* as it struck thin wooden paddles and *chack* when it leapt from the hard table surface. The rhythm pulsated steady as a metronome. Winners of ping-pong games skipped meals to hold control of the table. Waiting challengers decided if their hunger for a takeover outweighed a need for cafeteria nutrition.

It was early in the evening when the bus arrived back at camp after the first full day at the golf course. As Chad proceeded towards the sleeping lodge, he heard a ping-pong game start in the main hall. When he reached the bunk space, he noticed bed sheets missing on the adjacent top mattress.

The third boy sharing the cubicle entered. Chad asked him, "What happened to Cubby?" Charles was the fourth boy's real name, but he preferred Cubby.

Buzzy arrived and climbed up on the top bunk.

"He went home," replied the other boy named Steve. Because he vowed to skip showering all week, campers began calling him *Stinky* Steve. As the days grew, no one could stand to be around his oily hair and wreaking body odor. "He gets these migraine headaches outta nowhere," *Stinky* Steve said. "Doesn't know why. He said they lasted for days."

The night before, Chad learned *Stinky* Steve and Cubby attended golf camp the previous year and decided to be bunkmates this year.

"He started gettin' one at lunchtime," *Stinky* Steve said. He went to a counselor and they drove him back and his parents already came and got him."

"Um, too bad." Chad sympathized.

"Whatta chump," Buzzy said, rubbing fake tears from his eyes. "Had to go home to Mommy."

Stinky Steve shot Buzzy a dirty look.

Chad wondered how Buzzy would have reacted to his idea of going home early.

At dinner, numerous campers talked about the migraine headache sending Cubby home along with other stories of painful woes. Pounding hundreds of range balls and trampling for miles around the course took its toll. A wrath of blisters invaded the tender digits of all campers. Re-positioned grips wore on softer skin forming liquid-filled bubbles. More swings caused the pouch to break and the tenderness turned to pain. Band-Aids became a valuable commodity.

*   *   *

The orderliness of golf camp wore on Buzzy. At the lodge and on the golf course, counselors watched every move and adhered to a strict schedule. Pressure mounted to be on time and to pay attention. Buzzy struggled through instructional sessions and slogged around nine holes of golf in the morning and nine more in the afternoon. Golf camp included much more golf and a lot less camp than he expected.

Buzzy sported a Band-Aid on every finger and affixed them across the palms of both hands. For relief, he tweaked the practice range schedule by spending more time at the water jug watching others. The blistered hands thanked him for it.

What this crowd needed, Buzzy thought, *was lighter air*. Standing near the water jug, he decided to rededicate his time at camp to having fun. Minutes later, while the Crockpots learned the finer points of hitting a 3-wood, Buzzy let loose a little flatulence on the golfing cadavers, *"Fphlubbbubbbfphlubbubbb."* It was like the curtain going up on opening night. Act I received numerous smiles from the critical crowd of onlookers. Buzzy waved his hand in front of his nose. "Whew!" he said with a sour look. "Who was that?"

The golf instructor giving the lesson paused for the laughter to subside.

Buzzy slipped back over to the water cooler to launch Act II. While others toiled on the practice tee, he held a cone-shaped paper cup in his bandaged fingers and waited. With the counselors out of sight, he moved behind a Crockpot and gave mock instructions. "Keep your elbow straight there Johnny." He crumpled and tossed the cup to the ground. "Keep those legs moving," he said with his arms draped behind his back.

The Crockpots ate up the routine. Most of them stopped hitting balls to watch the show.

"Now that I have your attention," said Buzzy, imitating the instructor's voice. "Let me show you how to add a little power." Buzzy grabbed a 3-wood from a nearby camper. As they all watched, he stepped to a golf ball. "When you take it back here," Buzzy said, swinging the club backward, "you have to release some stored up power." With the club above his head, Buzzy squatted and released another methane bomb, *"Fffrrrummmphhh."*

The Crockpots chuckled.

Buzzy handed over the borrowed club. "That's how you get a little extra power, son."

Buzzy carried the act over to lunch. "Ladies and gentlemen," Buzzy stood and said. "Now for your dining pleasure..." He delivered a showcase of artificial blasts that included the following set list: *The Repeater*; *The Trumpet*; *The Squeaky Mouse*; *The Tug Boat Horn* (complete with an overhead pull in the air); the high-pitched *Leaky Balloon*; and, the low-pitched *Motorcycle Rumble* (complete with wrist rotating on a fake handlebar).

Some of the Hot Plates and a handful of Microwaves stopped to catch an encore.

*   *   *

An attractive feature of golf camp included the appearance and instruction from touring professionals. It gave campers a chance to meet golf royalty, and if lucky enough, get some one-to-one advice. Chad chose the particular week in camp because it included an appearance of his favorite player.

After lunch on Wednesday, campers reconvened on the hillside facing the driving range. Joe Doaks, parked next to his massive golf bag, greeted the crowd along with another touring professional. One of them started the hour-long program by hitting shots while the other sat in a director's chair with a microphone and made comments. Chad smiled as jokes and stories intermingled with the instructions. An exhibition round of nine holes was to follow the demonstration.

Round Bob Brown took the microphone and addressed the campers. "To reward good play during the week, we like to select a few campers to serve as caddies." With that, he called names from the crowd. Chad watched as larger, older boys emerged from the hill and sidled next to golf bags.

Before the announcement of his assignment, Joe Doaks grabbed the microphone and spoke up. "I hope you don't mind," he said, "but I've got my own caddy for this round." Joe looked around the crowd. "Where's *Stretch, Jr.*?"

Adrenaline shot through Chad. He stood and raised his hand.

"There you are," Joe said. "Well, come on over and be my caddy."

Chad beamed. "Yessir."

Joe continued entertaining. "This here is my backup caddy on tour in case my regular guy can't go."

The crowd laughed and Chad felt like saying, *"Awe shucks."*

As the crowd dispersed, Joe lifted his bag inside the tongs of a wheeled metal frame. "I like my caddies to use a pull-cart when I play nine holes. It makes it easier for me to grab the right club."

At first, the pull-cart felt a little embarrassing for Chad. An unwritten code of conduct permeated throughout the ranks that no one under the age of fifty should ever use a pull-cart. An exception for women and old men never applied to the young and strong. When he tried to move the heavy bag, Chad disregarded the implicit taboo.

Joe draped a full-length bath towel over Chad's shoulder. "Go dunk one end of it in that bucket over there," he said while pointing across the practice tee. "It'll help us keep things clean."

Chad returned with the dampened towel around his neck, grabbed the handle on the pull-cart, and followed Joe to the first tee.

Entertaining aspects of the demonstrations carried into the exhibition round. The two professionals appeared to have paired up with the counselors for a friendly wager, but they exchanged nothing more than barbs. Campers followed beside the pros and stood near each shot.

Throughout the round, Chad wiped soil from a club with the damp end of the towel and dried it with the other end. Most of the time, he pulled the cart behind him with an outstretched arm. Other times, he pushed it in front before coming to rest. On the putting green, Joe tossed Chad a golf ball and he rubbed with such vigor he almost polished off the white paint. Smudges of dirt would not impede a perfect roll on his watch.

Joe interacted with the campers. "You know how to always be happy?" Chad heard him say to one kid.

"How?"

"Stay humble. Golf will make you humble. No matter how good you are, golf will serve you up a little humility."

Halfway through the round, *Stinky* Steve crept next to Chad. "You're not a caddy," he said out of earshot of Joe Doaks. "You're just a rickshaw driver."

A few other campers laughed.

Chad ignored the comment but noticed that Buzzy went over and said something to *Stinky* Steve.

For most of the loop, Buzzy strode next to Chad as if pulling the clubs around the course himself. Sometimes he dashed ahead to help spot where the shot landed and made sure no one trampled near. At one point, he helped Chad maneuver the pull-cart over a curb. Another time he stayed behind to rake a sand bunker. He even offered to fetch soft drinks for player or caddy. When Chad saw him raise his arms to request silence, he remembered Buzzy's ambition to become a marshal.

As the round concluded, Chad didn't expect any kind of payment. Honor and experience were reward enough. So, it surprised him when Joe took off his golf glove and gave it to him. The memento exceeded any amount of cash.

Joe Doaks returned to the lodge with the campers and ate dinner at the table with *Round* Bob Brown. When it came time for him to leave, the crowd gave him a standing ovation. Slaps on the back and handshakes followed him to the door.

Chad shook his hand and thanked him. He couldn't believe he ever thought about quitting golf and going home.

*   *   *

While other groups began the next day on the practice range, the Crockpots headed for the tenth tee. Buzzy stood next to Chad as they waited and watched two groups tee off in front of them. Air temperature dropped during the early morning hours reducing its capacity to hold water vapor. The resulting dew blanketed the fairways and greens turning them into a shade of gray. After teeing off, Buzzy duplicated the player's footsteps ahead as if trailing tracks in the snow of an arctic expedition.

It didn't take a rain shower to test the waterproof aspects of Buzzy's shoes. Within a few steps in the dewy blades, a steady stream seeped through his sneakers. By the time he reached the fairway, his toes swam around in soggy socks.

Once the group reached the putting green, Buzzy attempted to decipher symbols on the surface. Remnants of lines tracing the previous putts cut through the vapory surface on their way to the hole. The instructions for his putt remained in a life-size atlas. Buzzy watched as Chad took his turn on the green. As the ball rolled, a rooster tail of water spun in the air like the wake behind a speedboat. It stopped four feet before reaching the hole.

Even with the extra information, Buzzy still took three strokes.

As Buzzy climbed a shaded path toward the next tee, the weight of his golf bag tugged at his shoulder and his wet feet slid in his shoes.

Gasoline-powered engines from a fleet of mowers roared on an adjacent fairway.

As he slogged through the swampy sod of the next hole, Buzzy found himself in a sand trap. As he took a stance in the bunker, he noticed something shiny in the adjacent grass. After taking a shot, he grabbed his bag and headed for the object. As he got closer, he noticed the sparkle came from the reflected sunlight in a steel shaft. Lying in the uncut blades surrounding the bunker was an abandoned golf club. As he picked it up, Buzzy assumed the club survived an overnight drenching. "Hey guys," he said, approaching the others. "Look what I found."

Buzzy took a few practice swings. His hands enjoyed the corded grip and forged iron head. "Sweet," he said as the clubhead cut through the wet grass. "I bet I can hit it a mile with this."

"Um, someone's probably, like, looking for it," Chad said.

"Maybe not."

"When we get in," Chad said. "You should like, turn it in."

Buzzy figured finders keepers. "What?"

"Yeah," Chad said. "What if you lost it? Wouldn't you, like, want someone else to find it, and turn it in for you?"

Buzzy never considered that before and slid the club into his bag.

By the time the group made it to the twelfth fairway, the noisy mowers emerged back at the tee. Having shaved the tops off dewy blades of grass on a routine basis, the crew operating the mowers covered the ground in an efficient manner. The gray, dew-covered grass awaited a fateful transformation from the spinning blades that would restore it back to green.

Midway through the thirteenth hole, Buzzy decided to surrender. He picked up his ball from the fairway and retreated to the shaded tree line. He watched two large mowers speed around the fairway while another mower, with its blades set higher, trimmed the rough. Ahead, a smaller one circled the green to shave the grass and extract moisture. The shapes and lines left by all the footsteps and tracks disappeared like a good shaking of an Etch-A-Sketch. Buzzy couldn't think of anything to say worth raising his voice over the deafening decibels.

As quickly as they appeared, the machines completed the work and vanished from sight. Grass clippings covered Buzzy's wet sneakers by the time he reached the green. Rolling putts across the surface returned to normal speed. *Just like that*, Buzzy thought, *mowers changed everything*.

When they finished the round, Buzzy approached a counselor. He pulled the lost club from his bag and handed it over. "I found this on the course."

The counselor gave him a smile. "Thanks." He stepped up on a bench and cupped his hands to his mouth. "Listen up," he said loud enough to get attention. "Which one of you knuckleheads is missing a sand wedge? Check your bags."

Iron clubs rattled in all the bags as campers scrambled to take a quick inventory. Buzzy watched as those with elaborate headcovers kept rotating them out of the way to get a correct count.

When no one responded, the young counselor made the announcement again. "While you're at it, everyone should be checking to see if any of your clubs are missing."

Buzzy held a glint of hope. He figured that if the club went unclaimed, it would revert to him.

"It's me," one kid yelled as if he heard a winning number in Bingo.

"Here ya' go," the counselor said, handing the club to the kid grip-end first. He made another announcement in a loud voice. "Let this be a reminder to the rest of you knuckleheads to keep up with your clubs." He pointed toward Buzzy. "You should thank this guy. He's the one that turned it in."

The kid approached Buzzy. "Wow," he said, shaking his head and sighing. "You don't know how much trouble I would've been in if I had lost this club. It's one of my dad's. I begged him to let me bring it to camp and promised I'd take good care of it. He's always telling me I'm not responsible and stuff. And, if I'd a lost it, he would've killed me."

"No problem," said Buzzy. "I know what you mean." And, for the first time ever, Buzzy did know what he meant. "You know," said Buzzy, wanting to make his effort even more heroic, "it probably would've got run over by a mower if it weren't for me."

"Thank you. Thank you," the kid said. If that were not enough, he added one more. "Thank you."

*   *   *

"Lights out in one hour," *Round* Bob Brown announced to the crowd as he wrapped up the evening program.

Chad waited with Buzzy to play a game of ping-pong, but time ran out before they got a chance. Chad returned to the bunk space, loaded his toothbrush, and made his way to the adjacent bathroom. Unlike the rebellious son or daughter of a minister, Chad made it a habit to practice the dental hygiene his father preached.

Buzzy claimed he forgot to pack a toothbrush.

When the lights went out, a few campers still stirred.

Outside the cabin, night sounds filtered through the screened windows accompanied by a cooling breeze. An orchestra of cicadas, frogs, and crickets started playing the pulsating repertoire at dusk and continued until dawn.

Inside the cabin, a few campers struggled with the mandate for silence. Someone decided to join the chorus of nature echoing throughout the lodge. A muffled, "Hoo, hoo," took wing from inside the lodge.

Chad's burgeoning smile made no noise.

"Ribbet, ribbet," came from a deep voice.

A few giggles flowed.

Just as it got quiet, a string of cat noises came. "Meow, meow, meeeeeow."

One brave camper tried to suggest silence. "Shushshshshsh."

Imitating a common house pet made it okay for someone with limited imagination to join with, "Moo, moooooo."

Streams of laughter gushed with each new sound effect.

As it got quiet again, the camper known for his belching prowess, decided to get involved. Chad remembered him competing with Buzzy at lunch. With only two gulps of air the kid could burp every letter in the alphabet. The belched word, "Crock," traveled around the darkened lodge followed by "pot."

Laughter poured out the windows and dribbled down the stairs.

Within thirty seconds, the lights poured on.

Since his bunk stood near the door, Chad saw the young counselor looming by the light switch. "Okay you knuckleheads," he said with a loud and authoritative voice. "Let's pipe down in here." He constantly searched for the inexplicable knucklehead. *"Who's the knucklehead that left the water running? Where's the knucklehead that left his golf clubs on the cart path? Who's the knucklehead that didn't clean up after dinner?"*

With calm restored, Chad saw the counselor turn for the doorway. The lights went off with a warning. "I don't wanna have to come back up here again."

Five minutes later mocked noises of nature re-sprouted. A goose imitation took flight with a series of "honks." Chad figured the next noise came from someone confusing the sound effects with that of an automobile as a medley of "beeps" resonated ending with an old-fashioned "ahh-ooo-gah".

Although amusing, laughter remained quelled. Just when Chad assumed peace settled over the lodge, he noticed the wire mesh supporting the mattress above him sag. Springs screeched and the bed shook. *"Ffrrrummmphhh."*

Hoots of laughter stirred the entire third floor.

Within seconds, a slap at the switch re-ignited the lights. This time Chad saw *Round* Bob Brown standing in a pair of pajama bottoms and a tee shirt. "Okay you wise guys," he growled. "This is your last warning."

Chad froze in the silence. He looked up and noticed the same stillness in the mattress springs looming above. If questioned, Chad decided he would play dumb.

"I better not have to come up here again," *Round* Bob Brown grumbled. As the lights went out again, he gave them one last chiding. "Problem with you guys is there are too many characters around here and not enough character."

Beyond a few straggling giggles, silence fell over the lodge.

*   *   *

Gloomy weather started to close in the next morning. As the Crockpots began their lesson in a practice sand bunker, an impending storm front appeared inevitable. Buzzy watched as Chad applied what he learned by exploding balls from the bunker. As they swapped spots in the sand, a light sprinkle began. Within minutes, the gulley washer chased them to the shelter of a nearby cart barn. Counselors took a headcount and distributed towels to dry off clubs, bags, arms, and legs. Umbrellas stood open for drying next to empty bags lining the wall. After an hour of waiting, the bus pulled up to the large bay door, campers loaded and returned to the lodge.

Round Bob Brown stood at the front of the bus, his barren dome dotted with raindrops. "We have extra reels of golf highlights for this reason," he said to the crowd. "We'll start showing them in the cafeteria in thirty minutes."

Buzzy poured off the bus behind Chad and ran for the shelter of the covered sidewalk. Passing the main hall, he heard the beginning of a ping-pong game.

"We're playing poker," a camper said to Buzzy. "You guys want in?" The games took place on the floor between bunks.

A jolt of excitement shot through Buzzy. "Yeah."

Although rules prohibited gambling, the sleeping lodge hosted numerous clandestine poker games during the week. Since playing card games fell within the limits of acceptable behavior, the activity itself did not raise suspicion. The stakes, usually the discretionary pocket change budgeted for such luxuries as junk food, rose large enough to frazzle nerves yet remained small enough as to not bring tears should all be lost. The difference between winning and losing meant a windfall or denial of sodas and candy from the vending machines.

Buzzy scraped together loose coins hidden next to his socks in a drawer. Twice during the week, he had not won or lost enough to matter. Arriving ahead of Chad, he wedged himself into a cozy space on the carpet and stacked the coins near his folded knees.

A camper pointed at Buzzy and said, "You be the *Lookout*."

Rain pounding on the roof muffled the sound of approaching footsteps of camp counselors bent on raiding their operation. Vigilance heightened.

"Okay," said Buzzy agreeing to be *Lookout*. He wiggled a little closer to the door.

Another person volunteered to be the *Raker*. To maintain an innocent front, the mounting piles of wagered coins often times required hiding. If the *Raker* got the signal from the *Lookout*, he swept all the coins amassed in the pot under a nearby pillow. For security purposes, the *Raker* sat on the nest of cash like a persistent hen and promised not to move even if prodded. If a raking occurred, all the other players knew to don an innocent look and ask a question like, *"You got any sixes?"* The other person would say, *"Go fish."*

Within the first ten minutes, Buzzy began losing at a rapid pace. A cold streak kept compounding the calamity and he approached total bankruptcy. In hopes of earning some of it back, he borrowed some money from Chad. Once he glanced at the next round of cards, he knew his luck had vanished.

Without fortune on his side, Buzzy decided to use another ploy. He decided to bluff his way to victory. With the confidence of a millionaire, he pushed in all his remaining coins. As the other players with weak hands folded, his confidence grew.

When Chad called his bluff, Buzzy's heart sank.

The strategy failed. He fooled them all except his friend.

Holding miserable cards too embarrassing to expose, Buzzy grew nervous.

With some pondering, a plan came to him.

Just before he had to show the cards, Buzzy stood and looked around the doorway. "I think I heard something," he said.

The *Raker* rose to his knees and hovered above the pot.

Seeing nothing, Buzzy turned to the crowd. "Naw," he said. "False alarm." A feeling of importance came over Buzzy. Center stage was his. Jumping at the opportunity to perform, he looked over at the light switch and pulled his shorts above his belly button. He squatted low and wobbled. He stuck out both elbows to feel larger, rounder, and more authoritative. In a deep grumpy voice, he did his best imitation. "Too many characters in here."

A few of the poker players began to laugh.

Buzzy fed on the attention and expanded the act. He slapped at the light switch on the wall. "Quiet down in here you knuckleheads!" He waddled like a duck in circles around the hallway separating sleeping spaces. "Too many characters," he said in a cranky voice. "Too many Crockpots."

Poker players bobbed on the floor with giggles.

Even Chad leaked a wry smile.

Buzzy snuck toward the door and peaked at the stairwell. He stiffened and said, "I think I hear somebody coming!" He collapsed to the carpet and put on an innocent, yet serious look.

Hearing the warning, the *Raker* dragged all the coins in the current pot under a nearby pillow.

Cards piled in a panic.

When seconds passed and no counselor arrived, Buzzy peered around the corner again. He looked to the group and shrugged his shoulders. "Guess it was another false alarm."

"Aw man," Chad said. "I had a full house."

Relief flowed through Buzzy. The distraction saved him from losing everything. "You did?" Buzzy decided to continue with the bluff. "Well I had four of a kind."

Chad said nothing more.

Buzzy took a deep breath before dealing the next hand.

*   *   *

Although something smelled rotten, Chad said nothing. After another four hands of poker, he watched Buzzy bet and loose all his money. Not long after that, the high-stakes poker game fizzled out.

"Let's go play some ping-pong," Buzzy said.

Chad stuffed the few coins from his pile into a pocket and followed down the stairs.

Like an incompetent sprinkler head, the driving rain drenched
the concrete slab under the covered walkway. In the main hall, a
throng of more than twenty other onlookers squirmed in folding
chairs on both sides of the ping-pong table. So that teams rotated
to their turn quicker, the self-governing crowd of contestants
lowered the total points required to win.

Chad sat next to Buzzy in the line of challengers. Whispers of
strategy circulated between teammates as the *chick-chack* echoed
through the hall. Taunts precluded the launch of serves and cheers
followed concluding winning points. Spectators at mid-table
followed the ball back and forth over the net swiveling their heads
in unison. After forty-five minutes of waiting, Chad and Buzzy
rose to take the challenger's side of the dark green slab.

Stinky Steve and another boy dethroned longstanding
champions and now served for the first point to defend the table.

"You know," Buzzy said to *Stinky* Steve. "You really should
take a shower." If that was not enough of a taunt, he backed up his
suggestion with a reason. "You're really starting to smell."

A few waiting spectators laughed with Buzzy.

"Too bad," said *Stinky* Steve while serving the ball over the
net. "You'll just have to live with it."

"You'll have time to take a shower after we win," Buzzy said.

Stinky Steve ignored the crowd. "Doubt it."

As they got closer to game point, a waiting challenger joined
in. "Hey Steve, here's a bar of soap."

Sweat built on the shiny forehead of *Stinky* Steve. He shifted
his weight as the ridicules from the crowd flung his way. Gnashing
his teeth, he served the ball toward the net and said, "Well at least
I'm not a freak of nature."

The ball traveled toward Buzzy.

Stinky Steve said, "At least I don't have alligator skin."

Buzzy kept his eyes on the approaching ball and returned it
over the net. "What are you talking about?"

Chad continued concentrating on the bouncing ball.

Stinky Steve hit the ball into the net. "I'm talking about your
handicapped friend there," he said, pointing at Chad.

The *chick-chack* stopped.

Time stopped.

Buzzy slammed his paddle on the table, lowered his head and charged. He swung his arm around the midsection of *Stinky* Steve and tackled him to the ground. Once he got him in a headlock, Buzzy whaled away with punches. Within seconds, a rolling ball of fury entangled the two boys with flailing limbs and growls not unlike a pair of pugilistic pups. Some campers ran from the main hall while others stayed on to cheer. As they wrestled around, folded chairs crashed to the floor and the ping-pong table rumbled several feet from its position.

Someone shouted from the front door. "Here comes a counselor."

It was enough for the combatants to separate. Their faces were flushed red as they heaved for air. Oily hair on *Stinky* Steve's head pointed in every direction.

"What's going on in here," the counselor said. "What's all the commotion?" The counselor surveyed the collapsed folding chairs and ping-pong table skidded aside. "You knuckleheads better not be fighting in here," he said. "You were warned on the first day. It's not tolerated. Who saw anything?"

No one responded.

Disappointed by the silence, the counselor asked again. "Is anyone going to tell me what's going on?"

Again, no one responded.

"No matter how it gets started," the counselor continued in a stern voice while making eye contact with each boy, "anyone fighting will automatically be sent home." He stopped and stared at both Buzzy and *Stinky* Steve. "Doesn't matter who started it," he continued staring at both of them, "you'll both go home."

As the counselor departed, *Stinky* Steve waited a few seconds before disappearing from the scene. Buzzy said nothing as Chad lifted chairs and placed them back into position around the table.

Within minutes, the *chick-chack* restarted.

*   *   *

At dinner, Buzzy stared at *Stinky* Steve from the opposite side of the room. By the time he and Chad reached the bunk area, they found *Stinky* Steve had packed his stuff and moved to an empty space on the second floor. Since he didn't want to get kicked out of camp, Buzzy decided to avoid any further confrontations. Not having *Stinky* Steve around helped. Not to mention, everyone on the third floor noticed an immediate improvement in air quality.

As a bunkmate, *Stinky* Steve must have caught a glimpse of the scars. Buzzy thought about Chad and the accident. He remembered the sleepover and images of the scars. *They were easy to forget because Chad always wore long pants.*

Just before lights out, Buzzy leaned over from his top bunk. "Chad," he said. "You know I'm sorry about what happened."

"You don't have to be sorry," he said. "He deserved it."

"No, not about the fight," Buzzy said. "I'm sorry about what happened behind the shed." Buzzy never meant anything more genuine.

A few seconds passed.

"I know," said Chad. "It was an accident."

The lights went out.

Buzzy settled into the bunk. At first, he wanted to talk about what happened behind the shed. He wanted to hear what Chad remembered and if he really didn't blame him for what happened. After a few seconds, a gentle kick from underneath the mattress nudged him. He leaned over again. "What is it?"

Chad whispered, "No more fighting or we'll have to go home."

"Yeah, I know," Buzzy said with a hushed voice, "but he deserved it."

"Hey Buzz," Chad whispered a few seconds later, "thanks."

Buzzy said, "He deserved it."

*   *   *

Chad sat next to Buzzy in the main hall. They both finished breakfast on Saturday morning and decided to challenge one last time for ping-pong supremacy. Chad spun a spare paddle in his hand. "I wish we could stay another week."

Buzzy smiled, "Yeah, I'm just getting the hang of this."

A few minutes later Chad looked toward the double doors and noticed his mom entering. He dropped the paddle and stood to greet both parents. "You're early," he said.

"Well," his mom said, smiling with watery eyes, "they said we could come anytime." She grabbed him like a mother bear hugging her cub.

Smothered in her arms, Chad mumbled, "It's not even eight o'clock yet."

After a few seconds she said, "We're right on time."

"We still have to, like, pack," Chad said.

"Hey Buzzy," she said. She even hugged him.

"Our stuff's upstairs." Chad pointed toward the sleeping lodge.

She draped her arm over his shoulders as they strolled. "Why, I think you've grown an inch," she said.

"We sure missed you," his dad said. "Looks like they've been feeding you well."

As they arrived in the bunk area, both boys gathered piles of dirty clothes.

Chad's mom tried to fold them. "We got your postcard yesterday," she said.

"You did?" Chad said. "I almost forgot."

"I figured you might have," she said. "I started to get worried."

"Well, um, at least you got it."

"Yes," she said, "and it made my day. I've been worried all week." She placed her palm on his forehead. "Are you feeling okay?"

"Yeah, sure."

"We've been waiting all week to hear from you and I read the postcard over and over."

Chad's dad said, "I told you it was nothing to worry about."

"Well, I couldn't help it," she said. "Something just didn't seem right about it. I hardly slept at all last night worrying about it. But now that I see you're okay, I'm somewhat relieved."

Chad looked at her and smiled. "The whole week's been awesome."

"I can see that now," she said, "but I'm still a little worried about what you wrote on the postcard."

"What I wrote?"

"Yeah," his mom looked serious. "What's this about you being a *crackpot*?"

age 14

Chad's mom began her nagging early. "Did you finish the extra credit report?" She stood over him at the kitchen table. Predawn darkness lingered outside the window.

"Yeah," Chad said. "I'll turn it in today."

"Let me read it," she said.

Chad clanged the spoon on the rim of his bowl. He stomped up the stairs and retrieved the one-page report on Bunker Hill. The paper crackled as he waved it in the air like a white flag of surrender.

"You shouldn't have waited until the last minute," she said, shaking her head. "You had the whole weekend."

"I know, I know." Chad turned his attention back to the bowl of cereal.

His mom turned to his dad. "Did you know he got a 'C' on a history test?"

He lowered the newspaper. "A 'C'?"

"Yeah. Thank goodness the teacher let him do some extra credit."

Still gripping the paper with both hands, his dad looked at him. "I thought you liked history?"

"Sometimes, it's, um, boring."

"Boring?"

"Yeah."

"Have you finished the English composition yet?" his mom asked.

"I'm, like, having a hard time finding something to write about."

"Why not write about golf camp last summer," his mom said. "Or how about that golf tournament you played in when you got home."

"The Schoolboy?"

"Yeah, didn't you play well?"

"Yeah, but, since it was the first time Buzzy ever played in the tournament, I figured that he might, like, write about it."

"That wouldn't matter."

"Plus, you remember, I wrote about that when I was a kid."

His dad lowered the newspaper again. "Well, if you think you're having a rough Monday morning, I've got something here for you to read." He passed it across the table.

Chad glanced at the folded paper. As he swallowed, the cereal left a cold trail in his throat and stomach. He read the following short column:

JOE DOAKS CHOKES

(Rocky Coast, California) - Local golfer Joe Doaks carried a three-stroke lead going into yesterday's final round of the Pacific Invitational only to falter in the end. It was the first time Doaks held the lead heading into Sunday and his final round of 77 was a meltdown of biblical proportion. Although he denied it, the nerves were visible in his round with numerous missed short putts and a drive that sailed out-of-bounds on the second hole.

"That's just golf," Doaks said. "I was ready for today just like I had been on Thursday, Friday, and Saturday of this week."

Doaks has been on tour for more than ten years after playing both his high school and college golf in our area.

"I felt good and was not nervous. It was a great tournament for me and I learned a lot about myself and I'm happy to have put myself in a position to win on Sunday."

As the golf season winds down, it looks like Doaks will have to wait another year for his first win on tour. He has had several near misses in his career, but has yet to break through with a victory. Some say this may have been his best chance to win and others are labeling him the best golfer to have never won a tournament.

Chad felt the disappointment. It evolved into anger aimed at the messengers. He fumed and thought, *What do sportswriters know? They don't know Joe. How many of them know what it's like to actually be in competition? How many of them know what the pressure is really like? They don't know pressure. How many of them know what the disappointment is really like? How many of them know what a good guy Joe Doaks really is? They don't know what he's like off the golf course. How many of them know that Joe Doaks really doesn't care what they think? Sportswriters don't know anything.*

*   *   *

"Let's go see Sally," Buzzy said after Chad opened the front door.

Chad was confused. "What?"

"You know," Buzzy said. "Walk to the S.D.I."

"Oh," Chad said. It took a few seconds to realize Buzzy had remembered *Don Quixote*. Thinking about the language, Chad tried to use more of the phrases. "Friend Buzzy, let us sally forth on an adventure."

Patches of snow piled by the plow lined the road to the Super Drive-In. Chad's mom gave permission for the trek as long as he bundled up with enough warm clothes to equal those on climbing expeditions up Mount Everest. On top of long underwear, Chad wore insulated ski pants, two layers of overcoats, gloves, hat, scarf, and waterproof boots with a fur lining.

Buzzy, in a light jacket, sneakers, and no hat, kicked at the piles of snow as they trekked.

Within a hundred yards from home, sweat flowed down the gulley of Chad's spine. He took off the gloves. "You think we'll have school tomorrow?"

"I hope not," Buzzy said.

"There isn't much snow left on the roads."

"I can fix that." Buzzy went over to a pile and kicked some of the icy debris into the street. It melted as soon as it hit the dark pavement.

"I think we'll be going back tomorrow," Chad said.

Halfway to the store, they noticed a patch of snow in a front yard. It looked like an oasis of white surrounded by brown dormant grass. A snowman stood in the island's center. Warmer daytime temperatures shrank the figure from its original stature, but the freezing nighttime temperatures grew a skin of ice.

"Watch this," Buzzy said as he took off running up the swale. At full speed, he dove at the center snowball as if making a tackle on the football field. As his shoulder hit the midsection, a crack appeared, but the snowman remained standing. Buzzy bounced off as if he ran into a fireplug.

Chad smiled. "Leave it alone," he said, thinking it had been a fair battle. "Um, some kids probably don't want you to knock it over."

Buzzy ignored him. "One more try." He backed up a few steps and charged like an angry bull closing in on a matador. This time he reached up with his arms and struck at the snowman's head. With the crack already in place, the weakened structure tilted enough to tip over and smash to the ground. For good measure, Buzzy stomped on the toppled piles of snow giggling all awhile.

Chad never broke stride. "Very mature."

Buzzy ran to catch up. "You don't think that was funny?"

"I don't know. Some little kid probably built it. He might not think so."

Buzzy shrugged his shoulders. "What do I care?"

Upon entering the Super Drive-In, Chad passed the displays of candy and headed straight for the magazine rack. Sweet treats that once motivated the voyages grew stale compared to the latest juicy news. Chad thumbed through pages of a golf magazine while Buzzy looked at motorcycles for sale in the classifieds. Chad consumed the latest on the golfing scene then made his way to the snack aisle. His appetite, no longer satisfied with bubble gum and baseball cards, had graduated to calorie-loaded baked goods. He paid at the counter and exited the store.

"Check this out," said Buzzy while sliding a fruit pie halfway out of its paper wrapper. "This is the best part," he bit into the sugar-glazed flaky crust. The syrupy mixture of fresh fruit filling oozed into his mouth.

"These are better," Chad said, separating the sealed seam of cellophane on a coconut-covered snowball. "Check this out." He took a bite far enough into the cake to reach the cream-filled center.

As they crossed the parking lot, a car pulled up behind them and a horn blew. Surprised, Chad turned to see Buzzy's older brother Wayne rolling down the window. "Hey scroats," he said, "hop in and I'll give ya' a ride. Wait 'til you see what I've been doin'."

When Buzzy opened the dented passenger-side door, it let out a barking noise. Buzzy lifted the latch and pushed the seat forward. Chad slid into the backseat. A deformed passenger side door was only one of many visible flaws on Wayne's scrap-metal heap. Years in the sun faded the paint job and rust consumed the fenders and wheel wells. On the inside, rooftop adhesive let loose of the sagging fabric and the developing crevasse on the dashboard looked like an earthquake fault line. Springs in the seats squeaked in unison with the worn-out shocks when potholes swallowed any of the balding tires.

Wayne hit the accelerator and the wheels spun as they left the parking lot.

Chad stared from the backseat in amazement. He watched as Buzzy reached for the knob on the radio. Bursts of music, static, and announcements from pitchmen shot from the speakers as the dial spun across the face. When he found a familiar tune, Buzzy cranked the volume and bounced on the front seat. Chad had never been in a vehicle without parental supervision. The freedom felt intoxicating.

Buzzy rolled down the passenger-side window. Due to sideswipe damage, it dropped only halfway. As he spit over the glass edge, part of the incidental spray rode the gushing air into the backseat.

"Hey," Chad shouted through the breeze, "you got me."

"Sorry," Buzzy said. He extended an arm out the window like an airplane wing. Twisting his wrist caused the wing to float up and down on the wind.

"Roll up that window scroat," Wayne yelled. "It's freezing outside."

Buzzy cranked the handle and the window inched higher. Unable to make a tight seal, the window continued whistling a one-note song.

Wayne grabbed a pack of cigarettes from his pocket and pushed in the knob on the dashboard. After the lighter popped out, he touched the glowing orange circular end to his cigarette and puffed.

As the car interior filled with smoke, Chad tried to hold his breath. He squinted to keep his eyes from burning.

Buzzy said nothing.

When Wayne made an unexpected turn from the main road, Chad began to worry.

After traveling less than half a mile, Wayne pulled into the entrance of the elementary school and drove to an empty parking lot behind the building. Circular patterns cut by tire tracks disturbed the serene snow.

"Ladies and gentlemen—," Wayne said into an invisible microphone in his hand, "—introducing the worlds greatest stockcar driver—Mister—Wayne—Odom." He hit the gas pedal with the cigarette dangling from his lips. As the car reached the icy patch, Wayne gave it more gas and spun the wheel. Snow and slush flew from the rear tires as the car skidded in circles.

In the backseat, Chad held tight with one hand braced on the door handle and the other wrapped around the unbuckled seatbelt.

In the front seat, Buzzy raised his hands as if daring a roller coaster to go faster.

Wayne became bolder. "Watch this." He mashed the pedal and flung the wheel right and left. He slammed on the brakes and threw the gearshift on the steering column into reverse.

As the car spun in reverse, the circular pattern grew.

Wayne lost control.

THUMP!

In unison with the thunderous wallop, the mottled hood bounced and wobbled.

Wayne mashed at the brakes, but it was too late.

Buzzy flashed a startled look on his face. "What was that?"

"I don't know," said Wayne looking puzzled. He stubbed his cigarette in the ashtray and exited the car.

Chad pushed the seat forward and exited behind Buzzy.

"Check it out," Buzzy said. "You hit a curb."

"Aw man," Wayne said. "It was buried in the snow." Worse news headed his way. As he went to inspect the front tire, he found it had lost all its air. "Aw man," he said again. "Musta caught the sidewall."

The world's greatest stockcar driver had run into a stationary obstacle in an empty parking lot.

Buzzy shook his head. "Whatta we do now?"

"The spare's in the trunk," Wayne said. "We gotta change it."

As to not alert his mom, Chad realized the need to get home. "Um, I have to get home Buzzy."

"I know," he said. "This won't take long."

"Um, well, just in case, I think I'm gonna walk from here."

"Suit yourself," Buzzy said, holding the spare tire in the snow. "But I bet we beat you back."

Chad shrugged his shoulders and headed for home. As he made his way past the front yard with the toppled snowman, he saw two little kids trying to put it together.

When he reached home, he found no signs of Buzzy or Wayne across the street.

"Your face is red," Chad's mom said at the backdoor. She sniffed the air as he shed the winter clothes. "You smell like cigarettes."

"It's from Wayne."

"Wayne?" She scratched her head. "What does Wayne have to do with anything?"

"He, um, like gave us a ride."

"But I saw you walk up."

Chad went into the whole story. He told her about Wayne picking them up. He told her about the donuts in the parking lot. And he told her about the flat tire and his decision to walk.

"Well," she said, "I hate to do it, but from now on, you're not allowed to ride in that car."

"But Mom." Chad didn't want to explain the ban to Buzzy. "It wasn't, like, that big a deal."

"I don't care. Riding with Wayne just doesn't sound that safe to me."

* * *

Chad's mom stood next to another chaperone outside the chartered bus. She held a clipboard and took a head count as rambunctious students loaded for the graduating eighth grade class fieldtrip. Once onboard, she took an empty seat near the front. The chatty students grew louder. En route, she turned around a few times to check on the passengers. Someone from the yearbook committee brought along a camera and took pictures. Closer to Chad, someone told a dirty joke she could not hear. At one point, singing broke out.

The amusement park, which garnered more student votes than the museum and local bakery, was a short ride from campus. As the bus entered the main entrance, clapping and shouts of joy squelched the singing. The principal stood and attempted to quiet the crowd.

"Listen up," he said, pushing down the air in front of him, "stay in your seats." He feigned a half-hearted warning. "We're not opening the door until everyone takes his or her seat and quiets down."

It took almost a minute for the volume to lower.

"Okay," the principal said, "that's a little better. Now, a few announcements. First, you're all expected to be on your best behavior. I don't want to hear any reports about any of you from anybody about any of you doing anything wrong. Understand?"

Students signaled with nods.

"Second," the principal said, "don't leave the park for any reason. If you need anything, look for one of the chaperones, that's what they're here for. Third, we're all meeting under the yellow pavilion for lunch at noon. Does anyone need directions?"

No one responded.

"Fourth, we'll be using the buddy system today," the principal said. "No one wanders off on his or her own. Pick a buddy and stay with that person. Know where your buddy is at all times. Is that clear?"

A few students nodded while several others mumbled, "Yes sir."

"Okay," the principal said as he swung the handle opening the door. "Have fun and remember, we've got chaperones spread around the park. They will be watching you."

Within seconds, an invasion of the amusement park was underway.

"See you later," Chad said to his mom as he strolled by with Buzzy and two other boys.

"I'll see you inside," she said.

As he entered the park, the mixture of options captivated Chad. For those interested in the thrills of amusement park rides, the theme park contained three roller coasters, a log ride, two Ferris wheels, a carousel, and other rides made popular at any state fair. Outdoor stages and air-conditioned theaters offered a variety of live entertainment to attract the tastes of a wide audience. One day was not enough time to catch half of the productions. Underneath seductive stalls, contestants vied in games of chance for a crack at the cache of stuffed animals hanging just out of reach. Mouth-watering aromas wafted from restaurants, concession stands, and pushcarts to entice hungry patrons.

Two hours after arrival, Chad found himself in front of an arcade clowning in funhouse mirrors with Buzzy and two other boys. They were all wearing train engineer hats. The striped denim brim on the forehead provided shade for the eyes like a baseball cap and fluffy fabric on top mushroomed like a chef's hat. Chad froze when he saw his mother approaching.

"Don't you all look like real train drivers," said Chad's mom, grabbing the bill of his hat and pulling it lower. "Where'd you get the hat?"

"Um, Jeff gave it to me."

"He did?"

"Yeah."

"Well, I hope it didn't cost too much," she said. "He shouldn't be spending his money on you."

Chad shrugged his shoulders.

The other boys continued to jump, lunge, and make faces in the mirrors.

"Well," she said, "we'll see you at lunch."

"Okay."

Chad found an empty mirror and stared at the reflection. Turning and taking a stance, he thought of only one thing. With an imaginary club in his hands, he began a slow golf swing while glancing at his distorted image. He studied the position of his feet and the amount of flex in his knees. Chad assumed the other boys ignored him because they had witnessed this same routine in front of mirrors in the school bathroom and hallways. In the middle of a second swing, one of the boys yelled out, "Let's go." The bulbous hats bobbed as they took off running to the next unexplored destination.

Just before noon, the students began funneling toward the yellow pavilion. The four boys made a grand entrance wearing the funny hats. Buzzy imitated the sound of a train whistle and mimicked the pulling of an imaginary cord to a steam whistle.

Most kids laughed.

After distributing box lunches, Chad's mom came over with a billfold in her hand. "How much were they?" she said to Jeff. "I'll pay for Chad's."

Jeff got a funny look on his face. "Don't worry about it," he said to her. "I got a discount."

Buzzy and the other boy laughed.

"You should save your money," she said, extending a few paper bills. "Take this for Chad's hat."

"Well—," Jeff hesitated at first, but relented, "—if you insist."

"Um, Mom," Chad said. "Can I talk to you, um, real quick before you give him any money?"

"Sure." She withdrew the bills.

Chad rose from the lunch table and directed his mother away from the other boys. "Jeff said he didn't, like, want any money."

"I know, but I wanted to give it to him anyway."

Chad fidgeted. "But, I'm not sure, I like, want this hat."

"What's going on?"

Chad looked around and saw no other option. "They like, stole the hats. Okay?"

"What?"

"I know it was, like, wrong," Chad said. "But they didn't tell me until we were already, like, wearing them."

*　　*　　*

Chad didn't tell his mother the whole truth; he wasn't exactly kept in the dark. Worse yet, Buzzy masterminded the scheme.

Chad remained outside the souvenir shop while Buzzy and the other boys grabbed the caps. Since he had not taken anything himself, Chad reasoned it might be okay. When Buzzy handed him the hat, Chad placed it upon his head and acted silly with the bunch.

When his mother first questioned him, Chad hoped she would drop it. And when he realized he had to come clean, he tried not to implicate Buzzy. Her questioning and insistence on paying for the stolen merchandise dug at his buried guilty feelings. A confession ensured the thieves wouldn't get away with her money too.

Realizing the buddy system made him an accessory to the crime, Chad visited the souvenir shop after lunch. He returned his hat to the rack and left without notifying the salesclerk or implicating anyone. He hoped the example would motivate others to return the hot merchandise.

They filed past the shop several more times, but none of the other hats found their way back to the rack.

On the return trip to school, the yearbook photographer found the train engineers irresistible and requested a group photo. The four boys crammed into the same bench seat and posed for the camera. When the photographer noticed Chad's hat missing, she asked, "Where's your hat?"

"I, like, took it back," said Chad. Although no one asked why, he offered an explanation anyway. "I didn't like it that much."

Chad's mom gave him a slight grin of reassurance and never mentioned it again.

When the class yearbook arrived a month later, Chad flipped to the fieldtrip page and saw a photo of four boys crammed into one seat. His three friends wore devious smiles and train engineer caps. Chad sat hat-less wearing a smile that looked more like contentment.

*   *   *

Chad sat next to Buzzy while Mrs. Odom explained selection criteria for cuts of meat, fresh vegetables, and bread from the bakery. Fine China adorned her formal dining room table accompanied by embroidered cloth napkins. If given the honor, Mrs. Odom said she would host foreign dignitaries in the same fashion. Since Buzzy spent the day with Chad at his country club, she insisted on returning the favor. "I wanted it to be nice for our guest," she explained.

Mr. Odom rolled his eyes and grunted. Anchored at the head of the table, he wore a Hawaiian shirt covered with a monotonous array of tropical flowers.

Mrs. Odom reappeared in the kitchen doorway. Chad noticed her dress. It looked like something she might wear to church.

"I'm waiting for the bread to warm," she said. She looked to Chad and said, "So, what's the country club like?"

"Um, we just joined," Chad said, "so, um, I'm like, just learning about the place myself." He hoped they wouldn't ask too many questions. Terms like *Bermuda, Nassau,* and *Calcutta* confused him. He had no explanation of how the exotic locales related to country club life.

An alarm sounded on a timer and Mrs. Odom returned to the kitchen. The oven door screeched open and slammed shut. She emerged with a plate loaded with fancy vegetables and Salisbury steak covered with gravy.

Instead of digging in, Chad waited for the other plates to arrive. His mother's orders echoed in his head, *"Make sure you use good manners and eat everything served."* When he noticed a helping of green bean casserole on his plate, he swallowed hard and stared at the side order of grief. He dreaded all green vegetables.

"It was wicked nice," Buzzy said. "Chad showed me around the clubhouse, and I saw this huge wall of trophies and stuff."

Chad remembered Buzzy wanting to explore the entire building. He became determined to survey the men's locker room after Chad told him they were too young to enter.

"There was this huge trophy for the club champion," Buzzy continued with the story.

Chad smiled. He explained earlier to Buzzy that the club champion was not a competition for every club in the bag. There was not a *7-iron Champion*, a *Sand Wedge Champion*, or a *Putter Champion*.

"You don't even need money there," Buzzy said. "All you have to do is sign your name."

Mr. Odom cleared his throat and pointed in the air. "That's where you're wrong."

"It's true," Buzzy said. "They gave away free tees in the pro-shop. And you should've seen the towels they had clipped on the ball washers. They were just as good as the towels on people's bags."

"Somebody's paying for all that stuff," Mr. Odom said through a mouthful of food.

"I even beat Chad today."

Surprised, Chad almost pulled a neck muscle turning to Buzzy.

Mr. Odom leaked a sly smile. "You did?"

"Well," Chad said, "not really."

"Yes I did," Buzzy said. "On that par-3 hole."

"Just because, you like, had a better score on one hole doesn't mean you beat me," Chad said. "And, um, plus I think you took a *mulligan*."

Buzzy sank lower in his chair. "Oh yeah," he said, "I guess you're right."

The green beans grew cold on Chad's plate while he prayed for the courage to consume them. When no one looked, he crammed a forkful of the lime-colored legumes into his mouth. They tasted like grasshopper guts. His eyes watered. He chewed faster and grabbed his glass of iced tea. After taking a sip, he crammed torn shreds of bread into his mouth. It took two more rounds of the same routine to clear the plate.

Mrs. Odom said, "What else did you boys do today?"

"I met some other guys on the driving range," Buzzy said. "They were all talkin' about going to golf camp."

Mr. Odom grumbled. "I hope you're not making any plans."

"Well," Buzzy hesitated. "Can I go?"

"We can't afford it this year," Mr. Odom said.

There was no explosion, no further cajoling, and no extended rants.

Mrs. Odom looked over at Chad's plate. "Why, you ate everything Chad."

"Yes ma'am," he said. "Thank you. It was delicious."

"Well," she said, "there's plenty more. Would you like more?"

"Um, no thank you, ma'am."

"You must've really liked my green bean casserole," she said. "Can I get you some more?"

Fear raced through Chad. He forced a smile. "Um, no thank you, ma'am."

*   *   *

Chad believed he saw a snowflake. Having finished his homework early, his eyes wandered from the television to the darkness outside the window. As he checked the spotlight beams shooting from the corner eave, his warm breath covered the cold glass with condensate. He heard his mom in the kitchen. She was talking on the telephone about school.

"No, that's not the problem," his mom said. "His first report card was pretty good. I'm worried more about him getting swallowed up there. They just don't seem to look out for kids like him. I don't feel like there's anyone at that school that's going to take an interest in how well he does."

Silent pauses interspersed when the conversation shifted to the other end.

"Well, it was his idea and we wanted him to have some input in the decision. He wanted to go to the same school as his friends."

Pause.

"I know that now, but we wanted him to be happy."

Chad's first semester at Sunnyside High School was less than spectacular. Buzzy abandoned the seat next to him on the school bus, and once on campus, different destinations between blaring bells sent them in opposite directions. They shared one class, physical education. Because their lockers were on the same floor, they passed each other in the hallway and ate lunch at the same table in the cafeteria.

"We're very involved," his mom said. "You have no idea. I've met all his teachers, and we work on homework every night."

Pause.

"I know. Everyday we learn something new. He tells us everything."

Chad searched through the window for signs of frozen flecks. He thought about the times he felt lost in the crowd at Sunnyside High School. He signed up for challenging courses but never raised his hand. Even the best teachers spoke in harsh tones directed toward disruptive students dominating classroom attention. Chad felt like he sat in the balcony watching an orchestra trying to lead the conductor. The shackles of forced attendance and term limits provoked lazy students to hatch escape plans and think of early release. Chad understood why some people related school to prison.

"Well, he knows we want him to change schools," his mother continued on the phone. "We've talked about it, and he's even agreed. *He's ready* to make the change."

Pause.

"No, it's not like it used to be when we were in school. You have no idea. Things are different."

Pause.

"Yeah, that's where we're thinking. I called the school and made an appointment with someone in admissions. Everyone we've talked to seems to think it's the best."

Pause.

"I'm not sure what it takes. But I know there's a process and they only accept a limited number of applicants."

Pause.

"I know, but we decided it would be money well spent."

Pause.

"Not only that, but he'll have plenty of time to adjust—whether he can start after Christmas or next fall."

Pause.

"I didn't know he went there."

Pause.

"Yeah, college is definitely in the plan."

Pause.

"I agree one hundred percent and we're also thinking he needs to be around other kids that are working toward college, you know, and have similar goals."

Once the conversation shifted to upcoming plans for the holidays and gossip regarding other family members, Chad lost interest and tuned out. After she hung up, he dropped into the kitchen. "Who was that?"

"Aunt Paula," she said. "I told her about our appointment next week."

"Oh," Chad said with a smile. He remembered to ask, "Is it supposed to snow tonight?"

* * *

A little more than a week later, Chad and his parents visited Chatsworth Academy. They drove through town, crossed a bridge, and followed a stacked-rock fence leading to a carved stone sign serving as a sentry. Tucked on the side of a hill, Chatsworth Academy grew from terrain bordered by a river on the east, a forested wildlife preserve to the west, and peaks of bare granite to the south. Brawny oak trees that took root from acorns germinated during the Civil War shaded stone buildings with slate roofs that rose from their foundations around the same time.

As they entered the administration building, Chad's mom spoke first to a woman sitting behind a polished cherry desk. "We have an appointment with Mr. Adams."

"Yes," said the woman looking at a schedule, "you must be the Ashworths."

"Yes."

"Please take a seat and I'll let him know you're here." She pointed over to a group of antiquated chairs with carved legs and leather upholstery secured by hundreds of worn decorative tacks.

"Try not to wrinkle your jacket," Chad's mom whispered as they took a seat. She licked a few fingers and slicked down the cowlick on Chad's head. While they waited, she went over all the points she wanted to discuss using the same hushed voice reserved for church.

An echo of footsteps grew from a hidden hallway. Mr. Adams appeared from around a portico column and acknowledged them with a sedated salutation. "It is with considerable delight that I extend my heartiest and most congenial welcome to you all."

Chad's mom offered her hand first.

"Thank you for seeing us," his dad said, surveying the surroundings.

After shaking, Chad stuffed his hands deep into his pockets.

The impeccable Mr. Adams stood tall and held his head tilted as if his chin repelled his chest like same ends of a bar magnet. He wore a blue blazer and striped tie. The school's emblem, stitched in colored silk, covered the left breast pocket. A steamroller could have flattened the cuffs of his cotton shirt and creased the straight lines in his dress pants. Sharp edges skated on the shiny tops of his loafers. He spoke with elaborate detail and used words most people would have to look up in a dictionary. He referred to Chad as 'Master Chad' and continued with the fancy talk. "Here, we cultivate genius and mental acuity with a rigid framework of scholarly curriculum and noble comportment demonstrable throughout flourishing generations of academics."

As they strolled around the hallowed halls, Chad did his best to soak in the surroundings. Looking down, he noticed worn concaved patterns in the marble flooring from a hundred years' worth of leather-soled foot traffic. Eons of students climbing the stairs wore similar bowl-shaped contours in the polished stone steps. Looking up, Chad noticed illuminated oil paintings lining the walls depicting past headmasters and distinguished faculty. The portraits, commissioned by leading artists and mounted in gilded frames, captured the spirit of the man and his contributions to Chatsworth Academy. Chad looked at Mr. Adams, compared his blue blazer to those on the canvases, and found the emblem on the breast pockets identical. Several words of Latin appeared below a shield and some branches of leaves. The same crest appeared on the school's letterhead and signs around campus. Of the words in the motto, the only one somewhat familiar to Chad was *Excelsior*.

"Our paramount obligation is to emanate learned entities that contribute nobly and honorably to humanity," said Mr. Adams.

Chad muted most of the academic presentation and perked up only when he heard things he found odd or entertaining. Instead of a cafeteria, he learned they ate meals in a *refectory*. Mr. Adams talked about vacation days as *exeats*. He called the restrooms *lavatories*, not to be confused with the *laboratories*. Mr. Adams pointed to *halls* instead of buildings and pronounced the surname of wealthy alumnus that bankrolled their construction. Open spaces on campus were not courtyards, plazas, or patios; Mr. Adams referred to these areas as *commons*. He pointed in the direction of an east commons, west commons, lower commons, and an upper commons. The only tolerable idea of a shortcut at Chatsworth Academy was the sidewalks that crisscrossed through the centers of the square-shaped commons.

"Here, we nourish young minds with an erudite and prominent faculty supported with state-of-the-art infrastructure," Mr. Adams said. "Associations burgeoned at Chatsworth Academy have endured for lifetimes."

Chad's mom hung on every word throughout the tour and even took along a notepad to scribble notes. Well-rehearsed answers from Mr. Adams appeased her most inquisitive requests. Upon hearing them, she nodded with approval.

They entered the gymnasium named after a celebrated alumnus that gave his life in World War II. Chad's dad said, "I played in this gym when I was in high school." His voice echoed off the bare wooden bleachers and the dusty banners hanging from the rafters.

Mr. Adams downplayed the pursuit of sporting activities and assured it was not a suitable reason for attending Chatsworth Academy.

A trophy case lined a wall in the gymnasium lobby. As they passed through, Chad's dad searched a shelf containing retired basketballs with the final score painted on their aging leather skin. "There it is," he said, pointing through the glass. "The City Championship." He shook his head. "We lost to Chatsworth in the semifinals."

While strolling the lengthy trophy case, Chad came upon a section for the golf team and stopped. Numerous gold-plated cups adorned the shelves and trophies stood at attention with silver golfers frozen in a backswing. Chad examined the dates and the matches won.

"The sport of golf is an acceptable extracurricular activity," Mr. Adams said. "And as exhibited herein, historically, our squad has grown accustomed to success."

As Mr. Adams droned with his parents, Chad looked through the trophy case and noticed the mirrored back wall and his full-length reflection shining through the awards. With golf on his mind, the urge came over him to check the swing. He stood sideways, flexed his knees, and started a slow take-away.

Chad took another swing and his mind wandered outside the gymnasium doors. He envisioned the commons, the connecting classrooms, and the dormitories. He pictured the old oak trees and the rambling river. He wanted to see the grounds his way. For that, the site required the launching of an imaginary golf ball.

A long iron shot took off on a low line drive that whistled through the wind. For the first hundred yards, the ball flew along the trimmed hedge and carved stone archways. The backdrop for the streaking white orb changed from ivy-colored green to crisp sky blue as it rose above the buildings. At its peak above the granite hilltops, it drew left and began an unhurried descent toward the lower commons landing softly in the middle of the crisscrossing walkways where an 'X' marked the spot.

Chad thought, *Excelsior*.

*   *   *

Chad's mom always brought up topical subjects at the dinner table. "Did the groundhog see its shadow today?"

"I just saw it on the news," Chad said. "They said he did."

His dad said, "So does that mean six more weeks of winter?"

"That's what they said," Chad said. He began demonstrating a level of maturity in conversations with his parents. To prove his brainpower, he pondered the criterion for Groundhog Day. "But I don't get it," Chad said. "If the groundhog, like, sees his shadow, that means, that the sun is out, right?"

Both parents nodded.

"And if the sun is out," Chad said, "that means like six more weeks of bad weather. But, um, think about it. If the sun is not out, and, um, he doesn't see his shadow, that means warm weather is on the way. So, um, if the weather is like good on Groundhog Day, the news is bad, and if the weather is bad, um, the news is good. Don't you think they got it backwards?"

"I never thought of that," his mom said. "But I guess you're right."

Chad nodded and sat a little higher.

"Your son has an interesting story," his mom said. She looked across the table. "Go ahead and tell him what you told me."

Chad wiped his mouth with a napkin. "I was over at Buzzy's house this afternoon when Wayne came home."

His dad scraped some scalloped potatoes from a platter. "What makes that interesting?"

"Well, it was like the first time he had been home in a while. And, he had a tattoo."

Chad's dad returned the platter to the table. "A tattoo?"

"Yep. And Buzzy's dad went ballistic."

"Ballistic?"

"Yep, he went on and on about how it was like a good thing he was no longer living under his roof, because if he did, he would, like, kick him out of the house. But Buzzy's mom wasn't really all that mad about it. She liked the tattoo."

"She liked it?"

"Yep. She said Wayne was old enough to do what he wanted, and for, like, everyone should leave him alone."

His mom jumped in. "Well, I better not ever catch you coming home with a tattoo. You certainly won't get my approval."

Chad nodded and smiled.

"Same goes for me," his dad said. "In my opinion, anyone who gets a tattoo basically says to the world they have no concept of what the word *forever* means."

"I agree," his mom said.

"There's only two ways I'll ever accept a tattoo in this house," his dad said. "One, is if it came from a box of Cracker Jacks. And two, if you were in a foreign land fighting on the front lines defending your country. Even then, you'd have to be on leave and have been drinking so much that your judgment was poor. And, the tattoo would have to say 'Mom' or your branch of the military."

His mom said, "I don't understand why anyone would deliberately disfigure their body."

Chad smiled and changed the subject. "Anything in the mail today?" For weeks, he waited for the acceptance letter from Chatsworth Academy and made daily sifts through the mail. With time, his enthusiasm lessened to the point he only brought it up at dinner.

His mom gave the usual answer. "Not today."

"You know," his dad said, "Granddad is a man of very few words. But when he gives advice to people, a lot of them listen. I want to tell you a story about something he told me when I was in high school that changed my whole outlook.

"I was just like you," his dad said, "when I was waiting to hear about a college scholarship. I talked to several different schools and liked most of them, but wasn't sure if I would get any offers. So, for weeks I was really anxious to know if I was going to be able to go to college and where it would be.

"What my dad said to me put me at ease," he said.

"It made *you* feel better?"

"It did," his dad said. "The simple advice has helped my outlook on life whenever I get to fretting about things or have anxious feelings."

"Are you gonna tell us what he said?"

"As I was sitting at the kitchen table," his dad said, "he walked through the room and hardly even looked at me. But when he was almost out of the room, he stopped and said, *'Don't sit by the phone'*, and then walked out of the kitchen.

"Pretty good advice huh?"

age 15

As the car idled in the driveway, Chad started to fret. He said to his mom, "I told him to be ready."

After a few seconds she said, "Go up and knock on the door."

Chad mumbled as he pushed open the passenger door, "I had a feeling he'd be running late." His summer routine at the country club kept him from seeing much of Buzzy. Whenever he did see him, it was usually from a distance and included just a wave. Two weeks before, they took time to talk in the street and both agreed to play in the Schoolboy.

After ringing the doorbell, Chad heard twisting tumblers releasing locks. A vacuum of air pulled against the storm door glass. Chad tried not to stare at Mrs. Odom standing in a bathrobe. "Um, is Buzzy ready?"

She looked surprised. "Ready for what?"

"We're playing in the Schoolboy today."

"You are?"

"He didn't tell you?"

"He may have, but I forgot. Come on in," she said. "He'll be right back. He went with Wayne to get some donuts."

Chad tried to control his anger. "Donuts?"

"Yeah, it's my birthday," she pulled at her collar, "and the boys said they would treat me to donuts for breakfast. They've been gone awhile, so they should be back any minute."

"Let me go tell my mom." Chad turned and headed down the steps.

"Tell her to come in and have a cup of coffee."

Chad thought, *A cup of coffee?* The schedule was already tight enough. A ten-minute ride to the golf course left plenty of time to sign-in, hit a few practice putts, get to the first tee, and be off at eight-thirty. His plans didn't include any snags from Buzzy. His mom shut off the car and they both went inside. Chad stationed himself near the front door while his mom disappeared into the kitchen.

Between watchful glances at the driveway, Chad paced in circles.

Mrs. Odom spoke from the other room. "Well, he doesn't see Wayne that much anymore. And when he woke him this morning he was so surprised. I think he just didn't remember the tournament."

"I, like, told him I needed to be there at eight o'clock."

"Don't worry. They should be pulling in the driveway any minute."

Chad continued to pace.

After about fifty laps up-and-down the carpet and fifty glances out the glass door, he saw Wayne's car pull into the driveway. "They're back!" Chad glanced at the clock. It was quarter past eight. He shoved at the storm door handle.

Buzzy hopped from the passenger seat with a crumpled donut box and played dumb. "I thought you told me eight-thirty?"

"I told you twice that we'd pick you up at seven forty-five," Chad said. "My tee time is before you. Remember?"

"Guess I forgot," Buzzy said. "Sorry 'bout that."

Wayne grabbed the donuts just before they entered the house. "Where you goin' scroat?"

"To play golf."

"I thought you quit."

"No."

"Well," Wayne said as they entered the kitchen. "I wanted you to help me move a washer and dryer today."

"He can't," Mrs. Odom said. "He's already promised Chad."

Buzzy looked at the floor. "Aw man."

Chad clenched his teeth. "Yeah, and we need to get going." He pointed with his thumb toward the door then headed in the same direction.

As he rode in the front seat, Chad watched the blinking clock on the dashboard. It was eight-thirty when he first spotted signs of golfers. The winding road through the city park leading to Short Hills Municipal Golf Course dissected a practice putting green from the first tee. His panic diminished once Chad realized neither of them would make their tee time. He only hoped they'd still be able to play in the tournament.

Chad spotted a friend from the country club near the first tee. "Let me out here!" As the car halted in mid-traffic, Chad jumped from the car and ran.

The country club friend turned. "Where were you?"

"Runnin' late," Chad said half out-of-breath.

"I told the starter you'd be here."

"What'd he say?"

"Said he couldn't wait. So he put someone else with us."

"I knew it." Chad took a deep breath.

"Looks like he put your name down, or at least moved you to the bottom of the list."

"Let me go check and see."

"He's got you with Mark Crowe. That should be fun. People call him *Birdie* 'cause he's a jailbird. You should have fun with that guy."

"I'll catch you guys later," said Chad, heading toward the table.

"I penciled you in at the bottom," the starter said to Chad. "But you still have to go to the clubhouse and check-in."

Chad hustled to the car. "We missed our tee times." He grabbed his clubs and said good-bye to his mother.

Buzzy followed alonside Chad. "Does that mean we can't play?"

"No," Chad said, fighting to control his anger, "it just means we have to play last."

* * *

Buzzy found a shady spot adjacent to the practice putting green. He stretched out on the grass and used his golf bag as a pillow.

Chad returned from the clubhouse. "The guy inside said it would be like an hour."

"So we're playing together now?"

"Looks like it." Chad sat on the edge of his golf bag. "Like I told you before, they had us in different groups because, um, we had different handicaps."

Buzzy plucked a blade of grass from the ground and stuck it in his mouth. "But we're playing together now?"

"Um, yeah."

Buzzy smiled. After a few minutes he said, "What's the deal with the 'For Sale' sign in your yard? Does that mean you're movin'?"

"I'm not sure yet." Chad looked up into the trees. "My parents said we were, like, 'testing the waters', whatever that means."

"It means you're moving." Buzzy said. "Why didn't you say anything?"

Chad looked toward the ground and shrugged his shoulders. "I, like, just found out myself."

"Yeah," Buzzy smirked. He spit out the blade of grass.

Chad continued to look at the ground. "You know how I told you about maybe going to another school?"

"Yeah."

"I got accepted."

"Now I know you're moving." Buzzy plucked another piece of grass and stuck it in his mouth.

It tasted bitter.

Buzzy stewed at a low boil. When the man with a megaphone
called them to the first tee, Buzzy tried to spit, but his mouth went
dry. When introduced to the other playing partners, a kid named
Sam and a longhaired guy named Mark, he shook hands and
listened as Chad gabbed about them going to the same school.
Buzzy continued to chew on a soggy blade of grass. He shook his
head and wondered when Chad had changed. He remembered
being surprised the day Wayne moved out. Now that Chad kept
secrets from him, the same feelings of abandonment resurfaced.
Buzzy said with a hushed voice, "We don't go to the same school
anymore."

Chad said nothing.

*   *   *

All the chatter about moving caused Chad to remember how he
once watched and waited for moving vans. He hoped they would
bring a friend. As he proceeded down the first fairway, he recalled
the day Buzzy moved into the neighborhood. They were both ten
years old.

*It was summertime, a Friday morning. Mom watched from a
window while I looked through another one. Across the street, a
tractor-trailer was backed up to the front porch. Like all the other
times, I remember asking, "You think they'll have kids my age?"*

*She shrugged her shoulders. "I don't know. We'll have to wait
and see." She always said that. "Wait and see."*

*I didn't wait long. Buzzy showed up on the front porch that
afternoon. Finding a friend in the neighborhood was like landing
a giant marlin.*

Chad stood over his ball in the first fairway and waited for the
group ahead to clear the green. His memory continued to linger.
Less than two weeks after Buzzy moved in, the accident happened.
Chad remembered how the day started with a chore he kept
putting off.

*After unplugging the aquarium pump, a curtain of bubbles
vanished. Standing on a desk chair, I drew back the long pajama*

sleeve and jiggled the water surface with my fingers. As I plunged
for the slimy filter, a black molly and an angelfish fluttered toward
the treasure chest. Overhead light swirled through the ripples and
flickered on a branchy piece of orange coral.*

*"Looks like the fish are getting along now," I remember yelling
downstairs to Mom. My fingers, swollen by magnification, felt
alien as they churned in the graveled bottom.*

Ding-dong. *The doorbell.*

*A submerged arm held me in custody. I yelled, "I betcha it's
Buzzy."*

*Flip-flops slapped across the tile floor as Mom neared the front
entrance. "I wouldn't take that bet."*

Ding-dong, ding-dong.

The lock rattled and the door hinges squeaked.

*"Hi, Buzzy," Mom said. "Come on in." She yelled up the
stairs. "C.J.! You've got company."*

I shed the pajama top and dried my arm with it.

*Buzzy's voice sounded different indoors. "Why'd you call him
C.J.?"*

*"We've got two Chads in this house," she said. "C.J. is short
for Chad Junior. It eliminates some confusion."*

"Oh."

"How's your mother doing?"

"Still unpacking."

"Tell her to call if she wants some help."

*I dumped any thoughts about the chores. "I told you it was
Buzzy." A few drops of water still clung to my elbow as I sat
halfway up the staircase to put on sneakers.*

"And I said I wouldn't bet against it," she said.

Buzzy gripped the door handle. "Ready?"

I hopped from the step. "Let's go."

*"Don't wander off too far." Mom started for the kitchen. "I'll
have lunch ready at noon."*

Buzzy pushed his way out the door.

I straddled the threshold. "What're we having?"

"How 'bout a Cowboy Cookout?"

Cowboy Cookout meant beans and franks warmed on the backyard grill. "Sounds good," I said, "but remember, no costumes."

"Invite Buzzy if you want."

"Maybe." I knew Buzzy had no interest in theme lunches.

Mom leaned from the kitchen door. "And please," she said, "stay out of the flower beds."

I took a deep breath and exhaled. I thought an inquisition would follow about unfinished chores, but a clean getaway appeared possible. The flimsy screen door screeched shut behind me.

"You gotta see something," Buzzy said.

"What?"

"I can't tell you, I have to show you. It's wicked."

I chased after him.

Neither of us stopped to look both ways as we raced across the street. Remembering the aquarium, I slowed. The fish, I forgot to plug in the pump. "Hang on," I said. "I gotta do something."

Several steps ahead, Buzzy stopped and turned around. "What's the matter?"

"I'll take care of it later." I accelerated to full speed.

The tail of Buzzy's shirt flapped in the breeze as we rounded the house and headed for the backyard. When Buzzy dashed toward the shed, I recalled our visit to the spot the day before and the secrets hidden there.

"You gotta see this." Buzzy pulled at my arm. "It's wicked."

Behind the shed, a green plastic army man stood guard on a concrete slab.

"Stay here." Buzzy disappeared around the corner.

I heard the flimsy aluminum door at the front of the shed screech in its track. Within seconds, Buzzy reappeared with a container of lighter fluid.

I stepped toward a pile of rusting lawn chairs still covered with morning dew. An acrid odor of rusting metal seeped from the outdoor furniture.

Buzzy flipped a childproof cap and began squirting some lighter fluid at the toy soldier's feet. "Watch this," Buzzy said. He pulled a book of matches from his pocket, struck one, and dropped it on the pool of fuel.

WHOOSH! A ball of flames erupted in a flash.

"Whoa," Buzzy said, backing away from the heat.

I shielded my face with both forearms. "Watch it!"

Black smoke from the burning plastic rose to my nose as the soldier's rifle tip bent toward the ground and dripped. Unable to endure the assault, the once proud figure transformed into the same green goop it was before it hit the mold.

"Isn't that cool?"

I scanned the area for witnesses. No one appeared around. "Yeah, I guess."

"Wait here." Buzzy disappeared again.

This time I heard the screen door slam at the back of the house. I grabbed a stick from the ground and tested the bubbling green goop as if it were cheese dip. The back door slammed again and Buzzy's footsteps scuffled through the grass.

"Check this out," said Buzzy holding a blue plastic cup.

I took another step back. "What's that for?"

"I wanna try something new."

I grabbed the chain link fence to my right and leaned against the pile of rusting furniture. I watched as Buzzy filled the plastic cup with lighter fluid, struck another match, and dropped it in the combustible liquid.

WHOOSH!

Buzzy danced with the blaze. "Wicked awesome!"

"Careful with that." I ducked and dodged flames like a boxer caught in the corner of the ring.

"My old man did this at a barbecue once," Buzzy said as he sprayed the fluid onto the flame.

Through the blaze, I saw Buzzy place the container of lighter fluid below his waist and squeeze.

"Look," Buzzy said. "I can pee fire." With each squeeze, he sent a stream of liquid flowing toward the growing flame.

The threatening blaze grew near.
I tried to block the heat with both hands.
Breathing became difficult.
Reality became a blurry nightmare: Buzzy twisting and turning
... rusting furniture barricade ... creeping flames ... holding breath
... Why doesn't Buzzy stop? ... bellowing heat ... green goop ... no
bubbles in the aquarium ... trapped ... plastic chemicals ... panic ...
swallowing smoke ... Jump! ... Why doesn't Buzzy stop? ... Cowboy
Cookout ... Jump! ... sinking in quicksand ... plug in the pump ...
cleared cup ... No! ... rim tipping ... splattering fuel ... Flames! ...
Buzzy saw a ghost...green goop...lady climbing fence...riding a
merry-go-round ... sneakers ruined ... metal shed swirling ...
smothering blanket ... fuzzy clouds, sharp grass, dirt ... swatting
flames ... sizzling bacon ... wrapped like a papoose ... darkness ...
Oh C.J.! ... rocking in a cradle ... Don't touch! ... darkness ... gag
... plug in the pump ... darkness ... sirens ... darkness.

*   *   *

Buzzy had never seen Mark Crowe before playing together in the Schoolboy. Yet, there was something familiar about him. He felt a bond with Mark Crowe. Buzzy laughed with him as they watched a nervous golfer on the first tee. On the second tee, when Mark related a tale about a one-armed psycho, Buzzy hung on every word. As they traipsed across the golf course, Buzzy admired Mark's blatant disregard for rules. *Paul Bunyan*, Buzzy thought, *Mark Crowe reminded him of Paul Bunyan.* Buzzy no longer felt alone. *Not Paul Bunyan*, he thought, *Mark Crowe was just like Wayne.*

"You should see my brother's car," said Buzzy, jogging to catch up with Mark. "It's a wicked Chevy."

"Got my own car," Mark said. "Use to be my granddad's."

"Ya drive it today?"

"Nah, I live close enough to walk."

"In nine months, I'm gettin' my license."

"You don't look that old."

"Well," Buzzy said, feeling a bit put down. "I am." Now he had something to prove.

Buzzy thought, *Nothing like dispensing a few curse words to prove I'm old enough.* After the next bad shot, he erupted with a molten flow of foul language. The act would shame most nightclub comedians and radio shock jockeys. If needed, Buzzy could raise the volume.

If cursing didn't gain attention, Buzzy devised another plan; he would cheat.

At the end of the third hole, Chad pulled the scorecard from his back pocket to record the scores. With pencil in hand, he addressed the group, "What did everybody have?"

Buzzy looked over at Mark and smiled. "Gimme a five."

"Yeah," Mark said with a nod. "Gimme a five too."

Buzzy believed he saw Mark wink in his direction.

Chad shook his head.

As they waited on another tee, Buzzy watched as Mark pulled out a pack of cigarettes. He approached his new friend, "Got an extra one man?"

Mark scratched his stringy hair. "Extra what?"

"Extra smoke." Buzzy stretched to stand a little taller.

"You don't smoke," Chad said.

That didn't matter. Nothing would stop Buzzy. Grabbing the cigarette and lighter, he proceeded to light up. After a swallow of smoke, he leaked a chortling cough. His lungs and throat burned. His eyes watered and he forced a change in his voice to sound relaxed.

Buzzy didn't care what anyone thought. He didn't care about Wayne moving out. He didn't care that Chad was moving away and going to a different school. No one cared about him, so it wouldn't matter what he did. It wouldn't matter if he decided to cheat on his score. It wouldn't matter if he smoked a cigarette. He didn't need anyone.

He could make new friends, like Mark Crowe.

* * *

Sam Parma, the fourth member of the group, claimed to have played only a few rounds of golf. With his worn sneakers, drooping tube socks, and baseball cap, Chad figured he was better suited for the sandlot. Striped range balls were stored behind the broken zipper of his tattered golf bag and black electrical tape wrapped around the used grip of his 3-wood. Chad guessed someone got him started in the right direction, but from that point his golf swing varied wildly. A few times his foot slipped. Other times he swung too hard. Chad assumed playing in the last group with a beginner was punishment enough for showing up late.

Chad overlooked simple infractions that would have counted against one of his friends at the country club. He accepted the role of mentor and figured Sam's rule violations were not on purpose. "Hey Sam—," Chad said, "—you know when you tee up your ball, you're supposed to be behind the markers." Chad pointed across with a flat hand as if resting it against an imaginary wall. "You get, like, two club lengths back from the markers," he said. "But not in front."

"Sorry about that," Sam Parma said. "Thanks."

Although Sam lacked some golf skills, it didn't keep him from having an impact on Chad. It happened on the par 5, fourth hole.

"I'm playing lousy," Chad said as they moved together from the tee.

"Looks like you're pretty good to me," Sam said.

Chad waited on the left side of the fairway for the group ahead to clear. The kind words gave him a lift, but were not profound enough to provide a permanent impression.

Sam continued to hack his ball down the right side. By the time he stopped, he ended up about fifty yards ahead of Chad.

Chad, disgusted by his poor play and the slowdown from a backlog of golfers, grew impatient. After seeing his friends from the country club on an adjacent hole, he wished the circumstances were different. It reminded him of the missed tee time and Buzzy's behavior. Chad started to tell Sam he was going to hit, but figured he was in no danger.

With careless impatience, Chad made a quick swing. The bottom edge of the club clipped the ball's midsection sending it on a low liner. Looking up, he realized the ball was flying opposite from where he had aimed. It was rocketing toward Sam. Chad tried to warn him. "Fore! Fore!"

Sam appeared oblivious to the oncoming missile. As it slammed into the upper portion of his arm, he lurched backward as if failing to break through the sturdiest of locked arms in a game of *Red Rover*. He winced and hopped while rubbing the point of impact.

Horror raced through Chad. He grabbed his golf bag and ran toward the kid. "Hey Sam, you okay?"

"Yeah," he said with a grimace. "Where'd that come from?"

"Oh man," Chad shook with nervous anxiety. "Didn't you, like, hear me yelling *fore*?"

Looking at the ground, the kid only shook his head.

He appeared to be okay.

Okay or not, Chad felt horrible. He knew Sam was a novice. He allowed his frustration to grow into impatience, indifference, and endangerment. Even though the kid appeared okay, Chad went overboard with the apologies. "Want me to carry your bag?"

"Nah," Sam said. "I got it."

For the rest of the day, Chad regretted the mishap. He felt horrible. His carelessness had harmed someone else. He thought about Buzzy and the accident behind the shed. At one point, Chad offered Sam the use of his clubs knowing it would violate the rules of golf.

*   *   *

Sweat dripped from Buzzy's nose as he stepped around the edge of a pond. A stretch of dry weather moved the waterline several feet from the natural shoreline. The bank looked like peanut butter. Bubbles percolated from the mysterious depths and ripples expanded after dragonflies touched lightly on the surface. Buzzy scouted for moving shadows and wished he had a fishing pole.

As he shuffled along the perimeter, Buzzy stumbled across a lone club lying in the thicket. He dumped his golf bag and glanced around. As he raised it from the grass, the shiny shaft reflected a gleam of sunlight. The clubhead, molded from solid brass, appeared unblemished and the grip was hardly worn. Buzzy lowered the club. He didn't want to raise suspicion. "Hey," he yelled ahead to Chad.

Chad turned, "Yeah?"

Buzzy reconsidered his opinion. "Never mind."

Mark drew near.

"Hey," Buzzy said to him, "check this out."

Mark grabbed the grip-end of the club and swung it a few times in the air. "Don't you already have a 7-iron?"

"Not as good as this one," Buzzy said, snatching back the prize. He wouldn't fall for any tricks to change his mind. *Finders keepers*, Buzzy thought as he slid the club into his bag.

Buzzy blamed the original owner for being careless and irresponsible. Maybe he should teach him a lesson by not turning it in. Maybe the club had hit bad shots all day and the owner decided to banish it. If that were the case, Buzzy decided he would be the one to adopt the stray. He would take better care of it.

As he waited on the next tee, Buzzy fought off boredom. He turned the bill of his cap backwards like a baseball catcher and shot a few streams of spit like a squirt gun. He plucked a blade of grass and stuck it in his mouth. When a cooing noise echoed from a nearby tree, he held his ear to the wind. "Hear that?"

"Yeah," Chad said with a smile. "It's a dove."

"That ain't no dove," Buzzy shot back. "It's an owl."

"It might sound like an owl, but it's a coo."

"That's no coo, coo," Buzzy demanded. "That's a hoo, hoo."

Chad shrugged his shoulders.

Buzzy drew a club from his bag and wedged the butt-end into his shoulder. He lifted the shaft toward the trees and stared down it like a gun barrel. He pulled at an imaginary trigger and puffed explosions from his cheeks.

Chad shook his head.

"You're so lucky," Buzzy said to Chad as they trudged to the next green.

Chad glared back. "Lucky?"

"Yeah," Buzzy said, pointing to Chad's tee shot on the green. "You couldn't hit that shot again if you had ten chances."

"Sure I could," said Chad, looking at the ground. "Don't you, like, give me any credit for practicing and playing all the time?"

"Practicing?" Buzzy continued. "The only reason you're any good at golf is because your dad is good at sports."

"That's not true."

"Golf, golf, golf," Buzzy said. "That's all you ever think about."

"That's not true either."

"Guess what?" Buzzy said. "I don't even like golf. I never liked golf." He swallowed hard. Seeing the damaging blows land, Buzzy piled it on. "The only reason I went with you on all those golf things is because my dad made me."

Chad lowered his head and said, "That's not true."

Buzzy knew the words that would hurt his friend.

So, he fired them.

*   *   *

Playing the Schoolboy with Buzzy proved ruinous for Chad. He cringed at every wild swing that ripped giant divots from the ground. After awhile, Chad felt much like the pot-marked earth. Each of Buzzy's damaging blows took a toll.

The cursing, cheating, cigarette-smoking Buzzy seemed like a stranger. Beginning with the late arrival and continuing with the defiant behavior, every sticky situation escalated upon itself. Chad felt like a stranger himself. For the first nine holes, his score ballooned to a range he hadn't endured in years. Every time his concentration wandered, his opportunities for success diminished.

At the country club, where an un-tucked shirttail drew attention from members and staff, Mark Crowe wouldn't make it past the gate. With his tank top, ripped jeans, and long hair he might get

along with the maintenance crew or be at home in the caddy
shack. Even with a haircut and change of clothes, he could aspire
to work as far as the valet service. A foot taller, Mark loomed over
everyone and looked like a hairy hooligan.

Chad's dismal playing partners were not the only factor
impacting the day. The clear blue sky of the morning took on an
invasion of stratus clouds until the flock swallowed the sun. By the
time the foursome reached the sixteenth hole, a storm rumbled in
the distance. An adult running the tournament approached the
group and gave them instructions. They were to listen for a siren
that would suspend play.

Halfway down the sixteenth hole, the hairy hooligan motioned
to the group. "Over here." He stood beyond the left rough with his
fingers entwined in a chain-link fence.

Chad followed Sam as they moved toward darkness on the
edge of the golf course. Below a rocky precipice, the rush of
automobile tires echoed on a highway.

The hairy hooligan announced, "Now you're gonna see a real
trick shot." Taking a golf ball from his bag, he dropped it away
from the fence. With a club in his hand, he aimed toward the
highway and made a swing. With solid contact, the white missile
soared over the boundary marker and descended to the middle of
the road below. Tires screeched as the ball narrowly missed a car.

Buzzy bounced next to the hairy hooligan with a smile of
delight.

Sam looked worried.

Chad found it baffling.

Swirling winds from the approaching storm swayed branches
on trees.

The hairy hooligan reached into his bag for another ball.

Buzzy stood next to him. "What are you going to do?"

"I'm humming one at the next car."

Angry clouds grumbled closer.

Sam's face turned red. His fierce eyes stared and his jaw
muscles bulged. As the hairy hooligan reared back to throw the
golf ball, Sam exploded. "Don't do it!"

Mark froze. Within seconds, he stood with clinched fists towering over Sam.

As Mark poked him in the chest, Sam's eyes watered and his lip began to quiver.

Without warning, Sam launched an overhead punch.

Although the punch landed, it had little effect. It appeared to infuriate Mark. He launched a ferocious and rapid retaliation.

Sam caught a one-two punch to the stomach and nose.

Great, Chad thought, *my first hockey brawl on a golf course.*

Buzzy drew a club from his bag and reared it back.

Before he started forward with it, Chad grabbed the end. "That's enough!"

The melee halted.

Sam retreated to his golf bag.

The hairy hooligan grabbed his clubs and took flight.

Deep breaths heaved from Chad's chest. He stared at Buzzy. "What were you going to do?"

Grasping opposite ends of the unsheathed golf club, Chad and Buzzy struggled in a tug of war.

"I was just going to break it up," Buzzy said, shrugging his shoulders.

"It didn't look like that to me." Chad looked at the club. It was an over-sized 7-iron with a brass head. Chad let go. "Where'd you get that club?"

Buzzy looked away. "None of your business."

Large drops of rain fell from the sky.

A siren went off in the distance suspending play in the Schoolboy.

*   *   *

Mark Crowe was almost out of sight when Chad drew the umbrella from his golf bag. Once it was unfurled, Buzzy joined him underneath it. They started for the clubhouse as Sam lagged behind. As the rain increased, their pace slowed.

"I can't believe the way you've acted today," Chad said.

Buzzy kept looking straight ahead. "What do you mean?"

"Cursing. Cheating. Smoking."

"Aw, that's nothing," Buzzy shook his head. "I was just goofing around. You used to laugh at my jokes."

As they slogged along a tree line, the rain blew sideways, drenching their legs and feet.

"Well, your goofing around has, like, gotten a little out of hand," Chad said.

"You do the same thing."

"That's not true," Chad looked over to Buzzy. "Your jokes have changed. You've changed."

"Changed?"

"Um, yeah."

Buzzy no longer avoided puddles; he trampled right through them. "I'll tell you who's changed, and that's you." Spittle flew from Buzzy's mouth. "You're the one who's changed; changing schools, going to a country club, moving."

Chad stayed silent for a few seconds. Determined not to let Buzzy turn the tables on him, he struck back, "When you looked like you were, like, getting ready to hit that kid with a club, I really couldn't believe it. What did he do to you?"

"That was nothing."

"Nothing?" Chad punched at the air with the balled-fist holding the umbrella. "I would've, like, tried to stop him." Chad stopped punching. "If it weren't for my legs."

Buzzy froze as a streak of lightning flashed in the distance. "How many times do I have to say I'm sorry?"

"I haven't heard you tell anybody you're sorry."

"Bull!" Buzzy shot back. "I've told you a million times how sorry I am."

"I'm not talking about me." Chad tried to control his anger. "I meant the kid you were about to swing a club at. And that kid on the first tee you were laughing at. And what about those people in the cars that almost got hit by a golf ball?"

"It wasn't me throwing golf balls," Buzzy shot back. "And by the way, I thought you were talking about being sorry for the accident."

"The accident?" Chad realized Buzzy jumbled his apologies. "If you haven't noticed, um, we're way past that."

"Then what's with you?"

"What you should be sorry about is how you've acted today. The things you've done. That's what you should be sorry about."

"Well. I'm sorry I'm not going to private school," Buzzy returned to attack mode. "I'm sorry I don't have fancy clothes and golf clubs. I'm sorry we're not rich. I'm sorry I'm not good enough for you."

Chad shook his head and looked at the ground. "Um, just forget it."

They slowed to hurdle a stream of storm runoff.

"Okay," Buzzy said. "So that we're clear on this, for the one-millionth time, I'm sorry about the accident."

"That's not what I was talking about," Chad said. "If you can't, like, understand what I'm saying, I don't know how else to—."

"No," Buzzy shot back. "Nothing is ever your fault. You're *Mr. Perfect*."

"I don't even know what you're talking about."

The slog toward the clubhouse turned silent.

*   *   *

Of all the years Buzzy had known him, Chad never complained about his legs. Like the scars, he kept the limits from the damage hidden. It surprised Buzzy when he used the legs as an excuse from entering the fray. Buzzy wasn't sure if he should be mad about Chad bringing it up, or feel sorry for him. Before they reached the clubhouse, Buzzy said in a low, calm voice, "It wasn't my fault."

The rain bounced off the umbrella and pounded the puddles around them.

Chad glanced over at him. "What wasn't your fault?"

"The accident."

Chad said, "I never blamed you for what happened."

Buzzy recalled the accident. He could see Chad jumping over the flames. He remembered the cup splashing and the flames shooting higher. He remembered the look on Chad's face as the fire engulfed him. He remembered his panicked run into the house. He remembered the years of feeling guilty about what happened. He wanted to forget the accident. He wanted to be free of the guilt. Staring at the ground, Buzzy said, "Why did you have to jump over the cup?"

Chad hung his head and replied, "I know."

Buzzy expected Chad to react with anger, but he remained calm. "If you would've just stayed put," Buzzy almost begged, "and not tried to jump over the cup, everything would've been fine."

"I know."

Buzzy looked to the distance. "We would have been okay."

"I never blamed you."

They were both soaked by the time they reached the clubhouse. Chad collapsed the umbrella as they stepped under a covered porch.

Buzzy dropped his wet clubs in a stall outside the clubhouse. He shook his head one last time. "All you had to do was not jump over the cup."

"I never blamed you."

* * *

"I got an idea," Chad's dad said, folding the recliner footrest underneath. "Instead of spending our Sunday afternoon watching golf on TV, why don't we go get in a quick nine?"

"Great idea." Chad hopped up. "It's way too nice to be sitting here."

Since school started, the burden of higher expectations at Chatsworth Academy began to weigh on Chad. *A round of golf*, he thought, *would be a nice break.*

His dad robbed a few clubs from a normal-size bag and stuffed them into a smaller bag to carry. "There's nothing like fresh air." He inhaled as they strolled down the first fairway. "Look at the size of those trees and look at those birds flying. You can't get that watching TV."

"You think they're going south?"

"I would if I could."

No groups in front slowed their progress and no one behind hurried their pace. They had the golf course to themselves.

"Take a *mulligan*," his dad said after a bad shot. "We're out here today just to have fun."

They relayed trivial observations on miscues hoping the self-analysis might prevent someone from repeating the same mistake.

"I pulled that one," Chad said.

Later on, his dad said, "I'm swinging way too fast."

"What do you think?"

"Play it out here," his dad said. "Remember this green breaks more than you think."

"You're about 140 yards out, but it's uphill and you got a little breeze in your face."

"Atta boy."

"Good one there."

Chad tended the flagstick while his dad fixed ball marks.

Long putts and chip shots coming to rest anywhere near the hole were granted '*gimme*' status.

Between the golf, they talked about other things.

"How's school?"

Chad relayed classroom activities.

"When are we going to move?"

His dad gave an update on the closing date and listed the pending repairs.

"Who do you think will play in the World Series?"

They talked about the teams and the batting averages of their favorite players.

"Are they playing preseason football?"

Sometimes, they talked without using words. A wave called off searches for lost balls or signified a clear path to continue. A fist pump saluted a good shot. Nods, shrugs, and the occasional arm around the shoulders commiserated wayward endeavors.

Smiles said the most.

They shared abundant smiles.

"Okay," his dad stood about ten feet off the eighteenth green. "Let's both chip one from here. And whoever's closest has to buy the other one a milkshake."

Chad said, "I already beat you at this."

"That one didn't count," his dad winked. "We didn't *shake* on it."

Their long shadows stretched across the entire eighteenth green. The gray sky reflected on the adjacent lake turning it into a shimmering pool of mercury. A cool breeze tickled the flag as they completed the round.

As promised, they stopped off in the clubhouse for a milkshake. Whooping and hollering of a large crowd greeted them. They sat at the last available table and became captivated with the crowd staring at images broadcast on the television. They added shouts of joy and applause. At the program conclusion, the crowd continued the celebration. Chad and his dad got home in time to watch additional highlights on the local news.

The next morning, Chad was eager to get the newspaper. He flipped through to the sports section, separated it, and read a front-page story:

WINNING STROKES FOR JOE DOAKS

(Sabal Palm, Florida) -- Local golfer Joe Doaks secured his first victory on the professional golf tour with a course record score of 62 on the last day of the Sun Coast Open. Going into the Sunday round, Doaks was five shots behind the leader and turned in a career round.

"That's just golf," Doaks said. "I was ready for today just like I had been on Thursday, Friday, and Saturday of this week. I felt good and was not nervous. It was a great tournament for me and I learned a lot about myself and I'm happy to have put myself in a position to win on Sunday."

The win comes after twelve years of toil on the professional tour for Doaks and should put to rest any doubters that he could win. Later, Doaks joked about having gone from being known around tour as 'Joe Blow' to now being addressed by some as 'Mr. Doaks'...

Chad thought, *What do sportswriters know?*

*   *   *

The move began on a Friday and extended over the weekend. Chad's mom spent the week before cleaning closets and packing boxes. Chad spent part of his evenings doing the same. Up to moving day, they drove across town twice a day to and from school. They both looked forward to a shorter commute.

"Make sure you wrap some newspaper around anything that's glass," she said, giving last minute instructions on Saturday morning. She wore a bandana and one of his dad's old dress shirts.

"The only glass I have is the aquarium," Chad said from his bedroom. Months before, the last of the fish had perished. Chad drained the water, washed stains from the glass, and tossed out the soiled cotton and charcoal from the filter. At the bottom of the empty aquarium, a sandwich bag holding the washed gravel waited beside the clear plastic filter and the pump was wrapped with its electrical cord. Once in the new house, Chad planned to set it up again with fresh fish. He yelled to his mom, "I could use one more box."

"Check the garage."

Among the stacks of boxes, Chad found one and returned to his bedroom. All the clothes from his closet and chest of drawers folded neatly in bags and the books and games stacked into other boxes. A few dusty items remained on a shelf.

The first item, a scorecard from his first round at the Schoolboy when he was twelve years old, was relegated to the garbage can. Compared to the disastrous day with Buzzy several weeks earlier, the memento of his first tournament round seemed insignificant.

Chad recalled his conversation with Buzzy under the umbrella. It was the first time they really talked about the accident. They rode home from the Schoolboy in silence.

Late in the summer, before school started, Chad waved and said from his driveway, "How's it going?"

Buzzy stood across the street in the graveled shoulder. "Okay."

Chad tried to keep the conversation light. "I haven't seen you lately. Where've you been hiding?"

"Nowhere really."

"Hey," Chad said, "I'm sorry about the way things turned out at the Schoolboy." Chad chose his words carefully. He offered an apology, but pointed no fingers.

Buzzy nodded his head. "Yeah," he said. "Me too."

Not much else transpired.

As the fading scorecard rested atop the pile of trash, Chad resolved to toss out any lingering bad feelings.

He pulled a school yearbook off the dusty shelf. Before putting it in the box, Chad flipped through to find the fieldtrip page. He recalled the amusement park fiasco and wondered why he ignored Buzzy's shortcomings. The train hat heist should have made him suspicious. He should have noticed the wrong side of Buzzy earlier. Maybe, their friendship should have never happened in the first place.

Next from the shelf came a framed photo of him standing in the backyard wearing the knickers, argyle socks, vest, and pancake hat. Chad looked young in the photo and remembered the dread he felt posing. *She was right*, Chad thought. *It was cute*. He recalled all the support his mom provided over the years. She worked tirelessly in caring for him. At times, her concern felt overbearing and restrictive, but it was also comforting and reassuring. Of all the other mothers he knew from friends and teammates, he decided he wouldn't trade his mom for any of them. Looking at the nostalgic golf clothes, he now understood the appeal and loaded it in the box.

The golf rulebook given to him by Joe Doaks came off the shelf next. He saved it as a reminder of his first lesson at the country club. Instead of thinking about Joe, Chad reflected on his dad. Although he footed the cost of equipment, driving range balls, lessons, and rounds of golf, it didn't compare to the value of time spent together. As he placed the rulebook in the box, Chad thought about the old college buddy. He realized friendships occur throughout entire lifetimes. Some may come and go, while others may last forever. Some have a big impact on your life while others may not. Chad remembered the holiday movie, *It's a Wonderful Life*, and what Clarence the angel wrote in George Bailey's book, *'No man is a failure who has friends.'*

Chad thumbed through some golf instruction books. He scanned a few pages and considered his relationship with golf. It was not a friendship, but it did give him something. It never showed up late, and waited for him whenever he was ready. If he wanted to devote hours at a time honing his skills on the course or the driving range, it was there. On rainy days and during the darkness of night, he read books and magazines about the game. Whenever he needed or wanted golf to be a part of his life, it was there. Limited to golf by doctor's orders, Chad found golf rewarding beyond his expectations. He would play for the rest of his life. In exchange, Chad gave golf his respect by following the rules and practicing good etiquette.

Chad knew golf could never be a substitute for human relationships. Golf gave and golf took away indiscriminately. Only a person can determine the difference between a good or bad day on the golf course. Golf provided a reflection of a person. If not for the accident, Chad doubted he would have looked into the golf mirror and found so much staring back at him.

Golf helped him heal.

He put the golf books in the box and reached for a pile of Slushie points torn from wax-paper cups. Never able to accumulate enough to redeem a prize, the shredded stack went into the garbage can. As they scattered into the bin like confetti, he remembered the numerous Super Drive-In adventures with Buzzy. It was Buzzy that showed him how to make money along the way. He thought about *Don Quixote*.

Chad untied the string from the tournament ticket stub dangling from a shelf bracket. He stuffed it inside a book and recalled seeing all the tour players up-close and the sound made by a golf ball cutting through the air. He smiled when he thought about Buzzy's plans of becoming a marshal.

A lone golf trophy stood as the last item on the shelf. Chad wiped some dust from it and read the inscription once again, *Crockpot Champion*. Chad recalled *Round* Bob Brown and his speech the last morning on the practice range. *"All week we've been mixing, stirring, and baking and we've come to the resulting meal that is a complete golfer. Now it is time to serve the dishes in the form of a tournament."* The competition included separate flights according to groups starting with the Crockpots and ending with the Microwaves. All week Chad had proven to be the best golfer among the Crockpots and nothing changed during the tournament. He finished four strokes ahead of his nearest competitor.

Buzzy tied for last.

Chad remembered the presentation ceremony the last night at camp and how much fun he had there. Again, he thought of Buzzy and all the times he made him laugh that week. He remembered how Buzzy took up for him against *Stinky* Steve and how sincere his apology had been afterward.

As he brought the loaded box from his room, Chad realized how many of his fondest memories included Buzzy.

Even though they seemed to be moving in different directions, Chad decided Buzzy had been a good friend.

As he added the box to a stack near the door, Chad said to his mother, "I'm gonna walk across the street."

"Don't be long," she said, "the movers are pulling out in fifteen minutes."

"Okay."

Chad looked up and down the street before jogging over to his neighbor's front porch. As he poked the button, he heard the doorbell inside.

Mrs. Odom opened the door. "Well, hello Chad."

"Hi Mrs. Odom, is Buzzy home?"

"No," she said. "He went with his dad to the hardware store. Do you want to wait for him? They're supposed to be home any minute now."

"I wish I could," Chad said, "but the movers are pulling out in five minutes. Just tell him I stopped by."

* * *

"Mom's taking one last walk through the house," Chad's dad said as they both stood in the driveway. "You wanna ride in the truck?"

Crammed into the overloaded passenger car didn't sound half as exciting to Chad as riding shotgun in the moving van. "Sure."

His dad approached the driver.

With a beckoning wave, the driver invited Chad to join him. As another mover slid to the center of the bench seat, Chad reached high for the passenger-side door handle and pulled it open. He grabbed the door armrest, lifted himself onto a side runner, and hurdled into the seat. After pulling the door close, he rolled down the window and rested his hand on the metal bar that extended the side-view mirror. The smell of sweaty movers occupied the cab. Looking down to his dad, Chad gave a wave and said good-bye.

For most of the trip, the cab remained quiet. "You're a lucky kid," the driver said, working the clutch to find the best gear. "It's a nice neighborhood you're moving to."

Chad smiled and nodded along with piston knocks of the diesel engine. As he glanced out the window, he realized a different perspective sitting high on the road. From the passenger seat, he saw the tops of hoods and could spot the contents in the back of pickup trucks. He thought about all the moving vans he used to watch as a kid and how he hoped each one would deliver someone his age. He wondered if anyone in the new neighborhood watched for moving trucks.

The trip across town stretched more than ten miles. Light traffic made it easier although the driver took it slow around corners and up hills. Since he didn't see either of his parents' cars pass them along the way, Chad assumed they stayed longer to tie up a few loose ends. Chad spotted the carved wooden sign, *'Hills of Shangri-La'* and said to the driver, "This is it."

The driver nodded.

From the entrance, the road rose in front of them. They passed manicured lawns, mature hardwood trees, and well-trained hedges. About halfway up the hill, Chad noticed a girl, around his age, in a spacious driveway. She wore a bathing suit top while washing a car. He tried to minimize the ogling as they passed.

Ahead, the street appeared to terminate into a wooded area, but as they got closer, the hidden bend in the road came into view and the climb continued. The driver pointed toward numbers on the mailbox and slowed the truck. He pulled through moss-covered stone pillars and climbed the driveway to a circular area outside of a double-car garage. The driver backed the truck toward the door, engaged the parking brake, and killed the engine.

Chad had visited the new house several times, but it looked different this day. Today, it became home. He hopped from the truck and strolled up a small hillside adjacent to the parking area. As the sunshine nourished a bed of fall flowers, Chad looked down the length of the street anticipating his parent's arrival. As the minutes passed, he soaked in the surrounding view.

Through the large oaks and maples, he spotted remote hilltops and valleys. It would be a matter of days before their foliage began its annual color change. In the distance, he saw a slow-moving cotton ball of a cloud. It appeared to be heeding a warning from a blinking red light atop a steel-structured radio tower. Below, he noticed pools of slate rooftops and brick chimney monuments. He smelled the sweet perfume spilling from white flowers on a nearby row of shrubs.

Chad's mind wandered to golf. He imagined a shot departing from the vantage point. With the great distance in front of him, he thought only of the driver, the 1-wood, the big dog. He could almost hear a 'crack' as the golf ball exploded from the clubface. From the hillside, it sliced through the gentle wind and flew in front of a changing backdrop that included the green leafs of summer and the bright yellows and reds of fall. Forecasting the surroundings with bare branches in winter or promising buds of spring became predictable as nightfall. The launch, a spectacle-filled event reserved for motorcycle daredevils, drove the make-believe orb on a low line through a small gap in the trees. As it passed through the center of a leafy doorway, the golf ball climbed into the clouds. The whirling dimples whistled as it carved a path through the sky.

It flew over the girl washing a car. She followed it through the air with an impressed look on her face.

It gained distance with a helping push from a tailwind. At its apex, it made a slight turn to the left and descended slow as a sunset.

It was perfect.

LaVergne, TN USA
16 July 2010
189770LV00002B/2/P